"Come see the moon," Cody said

If *that* didn't sound like an invitation to a kiss. Autumn hesitated, but her legs pushed her up and propelled her forward. He opened the screen and they stepped into the night.

The soft evening breeze smelled fresh. Overhead, the moon hung in the darkening sky like a giant golden ball.

Autumn stared in wonder. "How beautiful."

"Yeah." Cody said, looking at her instead of the moon, his heavy-lidded gaze making her shiver. After a moment, he returned his attention to the sky. "It's almost full tonight."

He stood far enough away that they weren't quite touching, yet close enough that she felt the heat from his body and smelled the clean scent of his shower soap.

Electricity zinged between them, almost palpable, and every cell in her body arched toward him in silent anticipation of his touch.

Nothing happened.

Which was for the best, yet her entire body screamed for her to kiss him. She had to get away from him before she did something really foolish, like wrap her arms around his neck and pull him into a kiss....

Dear Reader,

This is the third book of my miniseries set in Saddlers Prairie, a fictitious ranching town in Montana prairie country. For years I have been volunteering for a wonderful foster care agency, Treehouse (www.treehouse4kids.org/). Working with foster kids is rewarding, but also challenging, and I have so much respect for foster parents.

This story features Cody Naylor, a rancher and foster dad. Once a runaway teen, Cody was rescued from a collision course with self-destruction by a firm but caring foster dad. Now Cody is determined to pay forward his own good fortune by opening his ranch to foster boys—a job far more challenging than he ever anticipated. Finding a housekeeper to put up with the challenges is even more difficult.

Autumn Knowles has just returned to Saddlers Prairie and is looking for an office job. But fate intervenes in the form of one too many unpaid traffic tickets and a judge who…

I'm not about to spoil the story by telling you what happens. I hope you enjoy Cody and Autumn's story.

I always appreciate hearing from readers. Email me at ann@annroth.net, or write me c/o P.O. Box 25003, Seattle, WA 98165-1903. I invite you visit my website at www.annroth.net, where you can enter the monthly draw to win a free book! You'll also find my latest writing news, tips for aspiring writers and a delicious new recipe every month.

Happy reading!

Ann Roth

Her Rancher Hero

ANN ROTH

HARLEQUIN®

entertain, enrich, inspire™

To foster parents everywhere. Your care and dedication go a long way to helping foster kids grow into caring, productive adults.

Recycling programs for this product may not exist in your area.

ISBN-13: 978-0-373-75440-3

HER RANCHER HERO

ABOUT THE AUTHOR

Ann Roth lives in the greater Seattle area with her husband. After earning an MBA she worked as a banker and corporate trainer. She gave up the corporate life to write, and if they awarded PhDs in writing happily-ever-after stories, she'd surely have one.

Ann loves to hear from readers. You can write her at P.O. Box 25003, Seattle, WA 98165-1903 or email her at ann@annroth.net.

Books by Ann Roth

HARLEQUIN AMERICAN ROMANCE

AUTUMN'S CHOCOLATE ZUCCHINI BARS

Adapted from *The Zucchini Cookbook*
by Paula Simmons

1/2 cup butter, softened
1/2 cup vegetable oil
1 3/4 cups white sugar
2 eggs
1 tsp vanilla
1/2 cup sour milk
(To make add 1 tsp lemon juice to 1/2 cup whole or
2% milk. Let stand 5 minutes before using.)
2 1/2 cups unsifted flour
4 tbsp cocoa
Scant 1/2 tsp salt
1/2 tsp baking powder
1 tsp baking soda
1/2 tsp cinnamon
1/2 tsp cloves
2 cups finely diced (not shredded) zucchini
1/2 cup chocolate chips (or more!)

Preheat oven to 325°F.

Grease and flour a 9″ x 12″ x 2″ pan.

Using an electric mixer, cream butter, oil and sugar.
Add eggs, vanilla and sour milk. Beat on medium speed
for 2 minutes.

Mix together dry ingredients and add to creamed
mixture. Beat for 1–2 minutes, until well combined. Stir
in zucchini. Spoon batter into prepared pan. Sprinkle
with chocolate chips. Bake 40–45 minutes or until
toothpick or cake tester comes out clean and dry.

This is so moist, it doesn't need frosting!

Chapter One

Of all the stupid things Autumn Knowles had done, she'd never imagined she'd be riding in the backseat of Sheriff Bennett's car—or be hauled before Judge Niemeyer.

The tall man squinting at her through tortoiseshell glasses was every bit as imposing as she remembered. Wishing she still owned one of the nice summer dresses Teddy had bought her, and mad at herself for speeding in Saddlers Prairie when she knew better, she locked her shaking hands at her waist. "Hello, Judge Niemeyer."

"Autumn Knowles. Never thought to see you back in Saddlers Prairie." Tugging on his ear, the judge frowned at the sheaf of papers on his massive desk—papers relating to her. "Had to get yourself another speeding ticket, did you? Driving a car with expired tabs will cost you even more."

There was no point in arguing that hers had been the only car on the road, or that she wasn't the only person in town to speed. "It isn't my car," Autumn said. "It belongs to my mother. She loaned it to me while she and Jett tour the rodeo circuit." Within twenty-four hours of Autumn's arrival in town a few days earlier, her mom and her latest boyfriend had left. Heather had said Autumn could sleep on the Hide-A-Bed until she got back on her feet, and use the car while she was away.

"One of you needs to pay for the tabs or you'll get another citation." The judge shook his head. "You already have more outstanding traffic tickets than a prairie dog has fleas. I understand you owe a few merchants around town, too. You and your mom are like two peas in a pod."

Autumn stiffened. "I'm nothing like her."

Heather wouldn't care that Teddy was married. She would've kept every one of the gifts he'd bought her, and had called Autumn stupid for getting rid of them all. But Autumn had been too upset to think straight. Shortly after learning that Teddy already had a wife in Butte, she'd scribbled him a nasty note, pawned her engagement ring and bought a bus ticket back home.

She'd dumped the expensive clothes, purses and shoes at a thrift store near the bus depot, and had left Bozeman with only a battered suitcase containing toiletries, cutoffs and tops, and the clothes she was wearing the afternoon she'd left Saddlers Prairie to run off with Teddy: jeans, an Official Bruno Mars Hooligan T-shirt, and combat boots that were too hot for the sizzling August weather. An impulsive act she now regretted, if only because a nice outfit would score points with the judge.

His bushy eyebrows rose skeptically, and Autumn pulled her shoulders up straight, doing her best to look responsible and decent—worlds different from her mom.

"I have my high school diploma," she reminded him. Not Heather. The second Heather had turned sixteen, and gotten pregnant with Autumn, she'd dropped out of school. "My mother lives on welfare, but I've worked since I was sixteen. Twelve, if you count babysitting—often for your own kids, I might add. You thought I was a great babysitter."

"I'd almost forgotten about that," the judge agreed, looking thoughtful. "My wife and I always liked you."

Maybe he was softening. "I don't take handouts, either—I pay my own way," Autumn added proudly. "I'm a responsible woman."

"Responsible?" Judge Niemeyer snorted. "What about the half dozen or so businesses you still owe money to? And don't forget these outstanding traffic citations you left behind when you ran off."

Ashamed of her brash behavior, of her gullibility and of not taking care of her bills, Autumn hung her head. If she'd known that fateful day fifteen months ago what she knew now, she'd have taken the time to get to know Teddy better, instead of running off with him a scant two days after they'd met.

But he'd promised her a wedding and a custom-built house for the family they would raise together. She'd wanted that happily-ever-after dream so badly that she'd thrown away common sense and made a fool of herself.

Okay, maybe she *wasn't* so responsible back then. "A person can change," she said. "I came back, didn't I?"

Saddlers Prairie was her home, the town where she'd always lived—if you didn't count the time in Bozeman. She knew people here, and loved the rolling prairies. She wanted to spend the rest of her life here.

"I intend to pay back every penny I owe, Judge Niemeyer, just as soon as I find a job." This morning she'd even asked her old boss, Barb, if she could have her waitress job back at Barb's Café. But when Autumn had run off with Teddy, she'd quit with no notice, and Barb wasn't about to give her a second chance. "I'm sure I'll find something soon. Then you'll see how responsible I can be."

"A job. Hmm." The judge's eyes took on a shrewd glint. "I know just the place for you—the old Covey Ranch, now called Hope Ranch. It's a home for troubled teenage boys. Cody Naylor needs a temporary house-keeper, someone to cook and take care of the place until he hires someone permanently. Sixty days sounds fair."

Autumn hadn't seen Cody in years, but she remembered him. He was older than she was. He'd gone away to college and later had started a high-tech company in Silicon Valley. Every Christmas he returned to Saddlers Prairie to spend the holidays with Phil Covey, who owned Covey Ranch—except the year he'd spent the holidays with his girlfriend's family. That year, Phil had flown to California instead. Everyone in town had talked about it, wondering if Cody would marry her.

When Cody was in town, he and Phil had stopped in at Barb's a few times. Autumn had waited on them. Cody was handsome, smart and the richest, most successful man she'd ever met. He also thought he was better than she was. The big tips he'd left had felt more like charity.

After Phil had gotten sick, Cody came back, but he didn't eat at Barb's during any of Autumn's shifts. She hadn't seen him in ages.

What was he doing with a boys' home? The very idea of living with and keeping house for a bunch of troubled teenage boys was enough to ruin Autumn's already bad afternoon.

"I don't know anything about housekeeping on a ranch," she said. She didn't cook, either. "Plus I have no experience with boys with problems." She had enough troubles of her own.

"You just reminded me how great you were with my kids. This won't be that much different, except the boys are a few years older. There are four of them, ranging in age from fourteen to sixteen. This will be a good job for you."

Was he kidding? "I really don't think so," Autumn

said. "Surely there are other people who'd be more qualified."

The judge's suddenly deadpan expression puzzled her.
"Cody needs someone to fill in immediately. You're here
and you're available."

She chewed her lip. "I don't know—"

Judge Niemeyer sat up straight in his chair and looked
down at her. "You want to prove you're responsible? Take
the job."

"But I—"

He shook his finger at her, as in "be quiet and listen."
Autumn shut her mouth.

"The way I see it, you have three options. The first
is, complete sixty days of what we'll call 'community
service' at Hope Ranch. Only unlike the usual community service, with this job you'll get room, board and a
salary, and at the end of the sixty days, I'll consider all
your outstanding citations paid. You'll have to work out
the payment of your other debts yourself.

"Choice number two is to pay what you owe the
county within ten days. I'm guessing you don't have the
eleven hundred dollars owed—that includes fines and
accumulated interest. Which leads us to option number
three—spend those sixty days in jail."

Jail? Autumn winced. "I thought you liked me," she
said in a small voice.

"I do. That's why I'm sending you to the ranch. This
is your opportunity to help some boys in need and learn
something in the process. Someday you'll thank me."

Thank him? Autumn opened her mouth, but the judge
wasn't finished.

"You should also know," he continued, "that if you
agree to work at Hope Ranch, but don't stay the entire
sixty days, you will be obligated to pay all your traffic

fines the day you leave, or you will go to jail immediately."

Tough terms indeed. This man didn't trust her at all. Autumn bristled. "If I say I'll work there, I'll stay the full sixty days."

"I hope you mean that."

"I do!" Her voice had risen, and she sucked in a calming breath. "Why do you care so much about Hope Ranch?"

"Because Phil Covey was a dear friend of mine, and it was important to him and Cody to make this boys' ranch work."

"Was?" Autumn asked.

"Phil passed away about eight months ago."

She bowed her head. "I knew he was sick, but I thought he was holding steady." Unlike Cody, grandfatherly Phil had always been friendly toward her. "I'm sorry. I didn't know."

"We all are. The job starts Monday."

"But this is Friday afternoon," Autumn protested. "Don't you have to notify Cody first?"

"I'll do that as soon as you leave—provided you exercise some common sense and take the job. What do you say?"

The judge didn't leave her much choice. Autumn sighed. "Looks as if I'm spending the next sixty days at Hope Ranch."

SHORTLY AFTER LUNCH on Monday, Cody glanced at the four boys seated around him in the great room at Hope Ranch. Each of them had suffered through hard knocks that made his own lonely childhood look like easy street.

"I called this meeting because our temporary housekeeper will be here shortly, and I want to set some ground rules," he told them.

"What do we—" Noah's voice cracked, and he paused in embarrassment. He was the youngest of the group, and his hands and feet seemed enormous compared to the rest of him, reminding Cody of a growing puppy. "What do we need *more* rules for?"

"Because she's agreed to stay for sixty days and we don't want her to quit early."

Neither of the two previous ones had lasted half that long. Within three weeks of the boys' arrival at Hope Ranch, Mrs. Meadows, the housekeeper who'd been a fixture at the ranch since before Cody had arrived some eighteen years ago, had abruptly quit. Her replacement, Mrs. Clinton, a fiftysomething-year-old widow who'd taken care of a local ranching family for twenty years, had lasted a scant ten days. Word had spread about the teens and the challenges they presented, and Cody and the boys had been on their own for nearly three months.

Which wasn't exactly working out.

Ty, the oldest and the boy the others looked up to, snickered. At six foot three, he was built like a quarterback, but his sixteen-year-old mind hadn't caught up with his man-size body. "She must really be hurting for a job, because no one wants to work in a house filled with losers."

"Language," Cody chided, just as Phil had admonished him when he'd put himself down all those years ago. "Try that again."

"We're awesome—okay?" Ty rolled his eyes. "Why did she take the job, Cody? What's wrong with her? Does she even know about us?"

Cody had his friend, Judge Niemeyer, to thank for their new housekeeper, but the boys didn't need to know how the judge had forced Autumn's hand. "Yes, she knows this is a foster home for boys," he said, ignoring the other questions.

He wasn't at all convinced that Autumn would survive any longer than the previous two housekeepers, let alone last a full sixty days. But they needed someone to run the house while he found a permanent housekeeper, and he wanted the boys to give this their best shot.

"She's the only one you could get, right?" guessed Eric, a stocky fifteen-year-old with a deep voice and a bad case of acne.

The rhetorical question didn't require an answer. "Let's give her the benefit of the doubt, okay? Now, before she gets here, I want to cover those rules. Number one, no going through her private stuff. Number two—"

"What about *our* private stuff?" Ty crossed his arms. "She'd better stay away from that."

"Yeah," Eric added, his posture and scowl matching Ty's.

As usual, fourteen-year-old Justin, of mixed race and a few months older than Noah, was quiet. He'd been the first arrival at Hope Ranch after Cody had opened its doors four months ago. Justin kept mostly to himself and was always on alert, as if expecting a physical blow from somewhere.

Each of the boys met weekly with therapists in private sessions, but the therapy wasn't enough. If Phil were still alive, he'd know just what to do to help them feel safe, and coax them out of their protective shells. Phil's stern but loving hand had taught Cody that he mattered, and had saved his life in the process. He was determined to pay it forward by giving these boys the same chance at success, but hadn't realized what a challenge that would be.

"She'll be cleaning our bedrooms once a week," he said. "One of *our* rules for her is to respect everyone's privacy."

Ty's eyebrow rose. "She gets rules, too?"

Cody nodded. "That's only fair. Rule number two is no playing tricks on her. That means no snakes, worms or other bugs in the linen closets, no cow patties in the bathroom or anyplace else in the house, and no dye added to the laundry. Don't act sick unless you really are, and no animals of any kind in the house without my permission. No tricks, period. Everyone got that?"

He waited for their grudging nods. "Rule number three—if she asks you to do something, do it."

Eric narrowed his eyes, adopted a gangsta stance and broke into slang. "I ain't listenin' to no bit—chick."

Cody knew Eric had never joined a gang, but had flirted with the idea before coming here. He gave him a level look. "If you want respect from other people, you have to give it to them first. That means listening respectfully to me, to Autumn and to Doug—" the foreman of the ranch "—and when school starts next month, you listen respectfully to your teachers. You feel me?"

"What if Autumn asks us to do wack shi—crap?" Ty crossed his arms. "Because she will."

Cody ignored the boy's cocky expression. "Good question, Ty. If you have a problem with something Autumn asks you to do, you come see me. But you have to be respectful."

At his reluctant nod, Cody continued, "Rule number four—obey the first three rules. Any questions?"

Eric raised his hand. "What do you know about Autumn?"

"I met her when she used to waitress at Barb's Café but I haven't seen her in years." The few times Cody and

Phil had dined at Barb's during Phil's three-year battle with pancreatic cancer, Donna had served them. Cody remembered Autumn as a scrawny girl who wore heavy makeup, with punk-style dyed red hair and a boulder-size chip on her shoulder. He knew she had a deadbeat mother and had supported herself from an early age. Having once struggled to feed himself, he always left a big tip.

Cody didn't know much else about her, except that she had some outstanding traffic tickets and that she'd skipped out on her job, leaving Barb, who owned the restaurant and also served as the town mayor, high and dry. It was exactly the flaky kind of thing Cody's own mother would've done. *Had* done, the day she'd walked out on him and his dad.

The boys knew about his past. They didn't need to know about Autumn's. "She just moved back to Saddlers Prairie," he said.

"You said sixty days." Ty picked at a hole in the knee of his jeans. "How come she won't stay longer?"

"You'll have to ask her."

"She a good cook?" Eric asked.

"I don't know," Cody said, "but I'll bet she's a good sight better than any of us."

Since Mrs. Clinton's abrupt departure, he and the boys had tried their hands at putting together their own meals, with dismal results. If not for fast food, the prepared dinner selections at Spenser's General Store and Cody's barbecuing skills, they would have starved. He didn't even want to think about the housework they'd neglected. It was the last thing any of them wanted to tackle after a hard day's work. The place hadn't had a thorough cleaning in months.

"What kind of name is Autumn, anyway?" Noah asked.

Cody shrugged. "Maybe she was born in the fall."

"Like your ol' lady probably named you after a guy who built an ark." Eric threw back his head and laughed, though the harsh sound was more of a taunt.

Bristling, Noah jumped to his feet. His face contorted, and his hands curled into fists. "Shut the eff up, zit face!"

"You shut up." Eric rose, too, his cheeks scarlet.

They squared off like prizefighters in a ring. Adrenaline pumping, Cody slipped between them. "Sit back down, both of you," he warned in the quiet tone he'd learned from Phil, the voice that for all its softness packed an ominous wallop.

After trading murderous glares, the boys returned to their seats. Still standing, Cody blew out a relieved breath and addressed all four of them. "We don't settle our problems with our fists. What do we do instead?"

"Eff off, Cody," Noah all but spat.

Ty, Eric and Justin looked on with interest, but underneath their avid expressions loomed tension and fear. Even after four months, they expected Cody to strike them, or worse.

How long would it take before they realized he intended to kill them with kindness and understanding—not blows?

"That's not the answer I was looking for," he said without a trace of the frustration he felt. "In this house, we talk things ou—"

The doorbell chimed, and all heads jerked toward the front entry.

"That's Autumn now. You guys chill while I let her in. Remember, we want her to feel comfortable here so that she'll stay. Otherwise, this house might just fall down around our ears."

Chapter Two

"Wow, that's some house," Autumn's best friend murmured as they rolled up the driveway to Hope Ranch. Not about to pay for Heather's license tabs, Autumn had called Sherry for a ride. "Keeping that place tidy—you're talking a ton of work." Sherry shook her head. "It's a good thing you like to clean."

Autumn agreed. Cleaning was one thing she was good at, a skill she'd developed as a kid when she'd kept house for herself and Heather. "Thanks for taking your lunch hour to give me a ride, and thanks for changing your weekend plans with Shawn to hang out with me."

"I'll make it up to him tonight." Sherry winked. "Besides, he understands that I needed to hang out with my best friend in person. I'm glad you're home for good, and superglad you ditched that jerk Teddy. I *knew* he was too good to be true."

Autumn only wished *she* had known.

Never again, she silently vowed. No matter how good a man seemed at first, soon enough he would show his true colors and either leave on his own or do something unforgivable so she'd kick him out. The only person she could truly depend on was herself, and she wasn't ever going to forget that.

Sherry pulled to a stop and Autumn got out and retrieved her suitcase from the backseat. "I'll call you later."

"You'd better." Sherry's tires crunched over the gravel, spitting puffs of dust.

Not quite ready to face Cody or the boys who lived with him, Autumn studied the gracious ranch house. Unlike Heather and Jett's place, half of a duplex on the far side of town, here there was no peeling paint on the siding, no cracked windows and no sagging porch steps.

An enormous vegetable garden filled a large section of the front yard, and behind the house a barn and other outbuildings were visible. In the rolling fields beyond, cattle grazed under large shade trees, while ranch hands operated farm equipment and performed the other chores people did on ranches. Having visited a cattle ranch only twice in her life, both times as a little girl, Autumn had no idea exactly what kinds of chores.

The hot August sunlight burned her bare shoulders and she pulled her hair free from its elastic and made a fresh ponytail. The air was so dry she could barely swallow. Or maybe it was nerves. The judge had filled her in on the particulars of what housekeeping at the ranch entailed. Cleaning she could do, but cooking meals for a hungry man and four teenage boys worried her. Beyond frying a grilled cheese sandwich or shoving a prepared meal into the microwave, she had no experience cooking a meal. Also, she had no idea how to relate to the boys, or whether they'd accept her.

Over the weekend, her anxieties about her new job had only escalated enough that she'd seriously considered leaving town again. But where would she go, and how would she live? She wasn't exactly flush with cash. Besides, she wanted to live *here*. She would stick this out and prove to Judge Niemeyer and everyone else in

Saddlers Prairie that she was reliable and trustworthy, a good bet for any employer in town. That way, when her sixty days ended, she'd have no trouble landing a real job.

Jerking her suitcase along, Autumn made her way over the flagstone walkway that led to the generous covered porch. The wide wood steps and porch planking were painted a deep red-brown, with overhead fans, padded chairs and wicker tables adding a welcoming air.

Or would have, had she been visiting. While she worked here, she'd no doubt be expected to keep the porch swept and clean. As good as she was at cleaning, she'd never been responsible for such a big house, never mind males—who, in her experience, were generally slobs.

Autumn swallowed despite her parched throat. She dragged her suitcase up the stairs, squared her shoulders and rang the bell.

One nervous breath later, Cody opened the big wooden door and the screen. He wore faded jeans and a navy blue T-shirt, and seemed bigger than she remembered, with well-developed biceps and a broad chest. Big and solid, all man.

With a chin just prominent enough to give him a decisive air, a wide mouth and a straight, slightly oversize nose with a slight crook in the middle, he wasn't handsome in the usual sense. But he was darned good-looking.

He may have been a snob who'd barely glanced at her when he served him at Barb's, but Autumn had secretly always been attracted to him. Looking at him now, she admitted to herself that she still was.

She wasn't sure what he was thinking, but he gaped as if he'd never seen her before.

"Hi," she said, nerves making her voice higher than usual. She forced a smile. "It's me, Autumn Knowles."

"So it is. I hardly recognize you. You used to have red, spiky hair. You've grown up."

He didn't exactly smile, but his eyes beamed approval, the kind she'd gotten since she'd first sprouted breasts in eighth grade. Never from him, though. Apparently, he'd finally noticed she had curves.

His eyebrows drew together and his lips thinned. She supposed he wasn't exactly thrilled that she was his new housekeeper. He glanced at her suitcase. "Is this your only bag?"

She nodded. Saturday she'd dipped into the dwindling supply of cash she had left after pawning the diamond engagement ring, and driven with Sherry to Spenser's General Store, where she'd bought sandals, sneakers and a few new outfits. She'd tucked the remaining money—a paltry two hundred thirty dollars—into the dented, stainless steel coffee canister she'd found at Spenser's for 70 percent off. Once she had enough saved, she'd pay off all her debts. Then when she found a *real* job, she might even open a bank account.

"Come in and meet the boys." Cody reached for the suitcase.

Autumn brushed him aside. "I'll carry that."

He didn't listen, and they grabbed the grip at the same time. Her knuckles briefly scraped his before he let go and stepped back, but the damage was done.

Warmth that had nothing to do with the sweltering heat spread through her, and she knew she was blushing. After wiping her feet on the welcome mat, she stepped into the spacious foyer.

Cody shut the door and gestured toward a large room with clean, off-white walls, polished wood floors and patterned rugs. The coffee table looked like petrified wood, and colorful Native American weavings and Western-style paintings hung on the walls.

It was the kind of room Autumn had seen in the decorator magazines she'd scanned when she'd naively believed Teddy would marry her and build them a house.

Only in the magazines, there was no motley assortment of boys sprawled on the furniture. At first glance, three of them appeared to be relaxed, save for their wary expressions. The fourth, a wiry, mocha-skinned boy, reminded her of a hunted animal poised for flight, his body tense and his eyes narrowed and watchful.

"Meet Autumn Knowles, our new housekeeper," Cody said. He nodded, and the boys rose to their feet. As if she were a lady.

Self-conscious and uncomfortable—Autumn knew she was no lady—she slipped her hands into the rear pockets of her jeans. "You don't have to stand up for me. Please, sit down."

"After you." Cody waved to an empty armchair facing the boys.

As soon as she took her seat, they all followed suit.

"Why don't we go around the room and tell Autumn your names, where you're from and anything else you want her to know." Cody gestured at the long, L-shaped sofa, where an older-looking boy who was built like a football player sat very still. Like a cat, studying a fishbowl with Autumn in it. "You go first, Ty."

"I'm Ty, and I'm from Chi-Town." His gaze traveled over her. "How old are you, anyway?"

Rude as the question was, Autumn replied calmly. "I'll be twenty-seven at the end of October. How old are *you?*"

"Sixteen." Ty's eyelids lowered a fraction. "For an older woman, you're smokin'."

The comment caught her off guard, but she quickly

assumed the closed, nonchalant expression she'd first cultivated at fourteen, when Heather's then-boyfriend had come on to her. But not before Ty noticed her furious blush. He flashed her a cocky grin that withered under a glare from Cody.

"That's not an appropriate comment, Ty," he said. "Try again."

The boy's face darkened, and he muttered something unintelligible under his breath. He sat back and crossed his arms. "I'm Ty, and I'm from Chicago. Go, Cubs," he said as if he were reading listings from a phone book.

Autumn managed a polite smile. "Hey, Ty. I'm a Giants fan, myself."

She hoped for a reaction, a friendly hoot of disapproval or something. But Ty remained silent and his hostile expression didn't ease. He hated her.

Despite her mounting discomfort, she clung stubbornly to her smile.

Next, Cody nodded at a stocky boy with a pimply face, military-short hair, a sleeveless T-shirt and tattoos on his biceps. He was a good deal smaller than Ty, but looked to be about the same age. "I'm Eric from the Bronx, and I'm da bomb," he snarled like an angry rapper.

He didn't like her much, either. Intimidated but darned if she'd let on that she was, she leveled her gaze at him. "New York—cool. I've never been."

"Noah, and I used to live in Omaha. I'm four—" his voice cracked and his face reddened "—fourteen."

"Nice to meet you, Noah."

For her courtesy, Autumn received a dirty look.

"Justin. The hood. L.A. Fourteen," he muttered in bullet points. His big, brown eyes narrowed to hostile slits before he ducked his head.

Autumn fought to maintain her composure, and focused on remembering their names. And silently wondered whether jail might've been the better option.

CODY WATCHED WITH growing dismay as the boys introduced themselves to Autumn with the same unveiled animosity they'd shown Mrs. Meadows and Mrs. Clinton.

Either they hadn't listened during the meeting or they didn't care. They knew how badly Hope Ranch needed a housekeeper, having suffered through months without one. Autumn wasn't the ideal candidate, but at the moment she was all they had. Couldn't they cut her a break?

At least she held her own. She seemed to have pluck in spades, which was impressive, but no guarantee that she'd last any longer than her predecessors. Especially with the boys guaranteed to give her a hard time.

Introductions over, the room grew uncomfortably quiet, the boys sullen and silent. Autumn's mouth had thinned into its own sullen line, reminding Cody of the tough-looking girl he remembered from Barb's Café. She shot a furtive glance at the door, no doubt considering bolting. Someone needed to break the tension or she just might.

Cody gestured at the boys. "You have chores to do this afternoon, so you'd best get to them. I'll show Autumn around and let her get settled before she starts dinner."

"You want me to cook *tonight?*"

The panic that crossed her face baffled Cody. Had the boys scared her that much?

"When it comes to food, we're easy to please," he assured her.

As true as that was, he caught his breath and hoped his encompassing gaze warned the boys to play nice. To his relief, they all nodded.

"The pantry is full, there's plenty of ground beef in the

fridge and the boys will bring you vegetables and salad greens from the garden," he said. "See you later, guys."

No one moved until Ty grudgingly pushed himself to his feet. Eric, Noah and Justin quickly aped him. Without a word, the quartet plodded out of the room.

As soon as the boys disappeared down the hall, Autumn slumped dejectedly in her chair. "*That* didn't go very well."

Her bare, creamy shoulders begged for a man's reassuring squeeze. Cody glanced away. "They get nervous when they meet someone for the first time. You should've seen them when they met me. I've never felt so awkward or tense. They'll warm up." He hoped.

They hadn't warmed up to Mrs. Meadows or Mrs. Clinton, but Autumn was cuter and a lot younger. Seven years younger than Cody. Her age could be a huge advantage with the boys—provided they didn't scare her off.

"I wanted to warn you about them in advance," he said. "I tried to call you, but your cell phone was disconnected. I didn't know where you were staying, and had no way to reach you."

"I was at Heather's—my mom's. She doesn't have a landline. My ex-fiancé canceled my phone, but I got a new one over the weekend. If you have a pen, I'll give you the number. Not that you need it, since you know where to find me now."

She smiled at her little joke—genuinely smiled for the first time. Her whole face changed, and suddenly she looked softer and very pretty.

Cody slid his phone from his hip pocket. "I'd still like your number."

He realized he sounded as if he was interested in her, which he wasn't. His priority was to give the boys the same solid foundation Phil had given him. Between over-seeing the ranch and working with the boys, he had his hands too full for much else.

Besides, he and Autumn had nothing in common. He keyed in her number and then stood.

She followed suit, smoothing her top over her rounded hips. "I'm sorry about Phil," she said, her big eyes awash with sympathy. They were an interesting hazel color, something he'd never noticed when she'd worn heavy makeup. "There aren't a lot of decent men in the world, and he was one of the best."

Cody wondered at her comment about the lack of decent guys, but she'd just broken off an engagement. After his own breakup with Heidi, he'd been pretty jaded about women. "He was. You and I both have things to do this afternoon, so let's get started with the house tour. We're standing in the great room, where the boys and I have our group meetings, and where we relax after dinner."

"Those boys actually *relax?*"

Her lips twitched, coaxing out Cody's own grin. "Believe it or not, they sometimes do. You should know that Ty is the head honcho of sorts. Eric, Justin and Noah follow his lead, so if you want something done, Ty's your go-to kid."

"So I noticed. The other boys copied his attitude, and no one made a move unless he did."

That she'd paid such close attention surprised Cody. As a waitress at Barb's, she'd seemed distracted, in her own world. He'd always been amazed when she'd gotten the order right. "What else did you notice about the boys?" he asked.

"They're a tough crowd, that's for sure. Ty knows he's good-looking and uses his size to his advantage. Eric acts like some gang member spoiling for a fight, but he's sensitive about his acne. Noah's voice is changing, and that embarrasses him. But Justin seems the most wounded. I'll bet none of them opens up easily."

Marveling at her insights, Cody shook his head. "You already know their names and key things about each of them. I didn't catch on nearly as fast. I'm impressed."

Autumn shrugged. "Noticing and remembering the little things is a habit of mine, a survival technique of sorts."

His curiosity was piqued. But he needed to show her around and give her time to settle in before dinner. He also wanted to get outside and help with a leaky irrigation system that was giving Doug and the crew fits.

"The boys' bedrooms and bathroom are this way." He led her to the hall on the far side of the great room. "Cleaning supplies are in the utility room down the opposite hall, which I'll show you later. Do you have any questions right now?" he asked as they walked side by side.

Autumn nodded. "What happened to your software company?"

He hadn't expected a personal question, but he didn't mind answering. "I sold it."

"Judge Niemeyer mentioned that you and your girlfriend broke up. Was it because you moved back to Saddlers Prairie?"

Cody's past was no big secret. "We broke up several months before that because she was more interested in my money than me." As badly as finding that out had hurt at the time, he counted himself lucky that he hadn't made a huge mistake and proposed to her. "Is there anything else you want to know about me?" he asked, his mouth quirking.

"Why did you decide to open up a ranch for troubled boys?"

"Because Phil took me in when I had no one, and now it's my turn to pay it forward."

She frowned. "Phil took you in?"

"That's right. When I came to Covey Ranch, I was a high school dropout and runaway."

"I had no idea," Autumn said. "What happened, if you don't mind my asking?"

"Long story short, when I was six years old, living in Phoenix with my parents, my mother ran away with one of her coworkers. She abandoned my dad and me." Cody had shared the story so many times he barely felt the loneliness and pain anymore.

"My father coped by burying himself in work and mostly forgot I existed," he went on. "Then he died. No one was able to locate my mother, and I didn't have any other family. I overheard two social workers talking about putting me into the foster care system, and I wanted no part of that. An hour after the funeral service, I took off."

He paused, checking to see if the story bored Autumn, but she seemed interested.

"I was headed for Canada and made it as far as Saddlers Prairie before my cash ran out," he said. "I was hungry and needed a place to sleep, so I sneaked onto Phil's ranch and raided the chicken coop. I was in the barn, trying to figure out what to do with the squawking chicken, when Phil caught me."

Cody remembered that night as if it was yesterday. He'd been scared spitless that Phil would turn him in to the cops. Or worse.

Autumn's expression was one of pure sympathy. "How old were you?"

"Barely sixteen and headed for trouble. If Phil hadn't taken me in and become my foster dad, I'd either be in jail or dead." Cody grimaced at the thought. "Thanks to him, I reenrolled in high school and graduated with decent grades. He loaned me the money for college, and encouraged me to start the software company."

"To think that one person completely changed your life... You're very lucky, Cody. Do the boys know about this?"

"All of it. Most everyone in town has heard my story."

"Not me."

"Well, now you're all caught up."

Autumn nodded thoughtfully. "And here I always thought you were a rich snob."

Cody frowned. "Where'd you get an idea like that?"

"You left me those big tips for no reason, like I was some charity case."

"You thought wrong," he said, stung. "I was trying to... Never mind." He jerked his head at the closest of the two closed bedroom doors. "This is where Noah and Justin bunk. Ty and Eric are in the other bedroom. They share the bathroom across the hall. Clean towels and bedding are in the linen closet."

"Don't be angry with me, Cody. You asked."

"I'm not angry, Autumn, just confused. Why would you think I was a snob?"

"Because you never looked at me when you ordered your meals. No one likes to feel like they're somehow inferior, and by not looking at me, that was the message you sent."

Her words struck a cord deep within him. How many times had he felt invisible when he was growing up? How many times had Justin, Eric, Noah and Ty? That he'd treated Autumn like that...

"I see you now," he said, looking straight at her. "And I hear you."

Some of her tension seemed to drain away, and a for-giving softness replaced the stony glint in her eyes.

She gestured at the boys' rooms. "I see they keep their doors closed. Is that to hide the mess inside?"

"In general they're a pretty tidy bunch. But they're teenagers, and they need their privacy."

"Will they mind if I go in to clean?" she asked.

"It means they don't have to do it, so no. They know you'll be going in once a week to change the sheets, vacuum and dust. I ask that you respect their privacy. In other words, clean but don't snoop."

"I'd never do that. Heather used to snoop through my stuff." Autumn made a face.

"That couldn't have been fun."

"You try living with a mom who considers you the competition." Autumn scoffed. "The men in her life were twice my age, and mostly losers. That's why I moved out when I was still in high school."

Cody hadn't known about any of that. "It took cour-age to move out," he said. "Supporting yourself at that age and getting through high school couldn't have been easy. How did you do it?"

"The same way anyone would—by putting one foot in front of the other."

She seemed so matter-of-fact about what she'd ac-complished, as if any kid in her situation would have finished school.

From his own personal experience, Cody knew better. He admired her for what she'd done. Autumn Knowles had more grit than he'd ever guessed.

Chapter Three

Autumn followed Cody up the wide staircase to a large, open hallway. Natural beam ceilings and skylights gave the area a bright, airy feel, and thick beige carpeting muffled their footsteps.

"My office is to the left, and my bedroom suite is straight ahead," Cody said, gesturing as he spoke.

The office contained the usual bookshelves, file cabinets, desk and several computer devices. Aside from a few scattered papers on the desk and a full wastebasket, the room was neat enough. Nice to know he wasn't a slob.

"What would you like me to do in here?" she asked.

"Dust, vacuum, empty the trash."

The entry to the bedroom was wide enough for them to comfortably enter side by side, but Cody stood back and nodded for her to enter first.

Although it was just part of the tour, stepping into his bedroom felt awfully personal. Autumn hesitated. This was where he'd bring his lovers.

"Autumn?"

Prodded by his puzzled frown, she crossed the threshold into a bedroom that was easily twice the size of any she'd ever seen. She noted beamed ceilings, interesting art on the walls and the sliding door to a balcony that overlooked acres and acres of rolling ranch land, before her unwitting gaze homed in on the king-size bed and the skylight directly above it.

She didn't so much as glance at Cody, but she felt his eyes on her.

She turned to him with deliberate indifference, and could tell by his neutral expression that he wasn't any more interested in her than he'd ever been. Was that relief she felt, or disappointment?

"Did Phil design this suite?" she asked.

"Yes, and the whole house as well—all for his wife, Sylvia. After she died, he was too grief-stricken to sleep up here. He moved downstairs and slept in the room Ty and Eric share now."

"Do you feel weird, sleeping in their old bedroom?" Autumn asked.

"I did at first, but when I came home to take care of Phil, he insisted I move into the suite. He said that if Sylvia had been alive to meet me, she would've wanted me to stay up here."

Cody looked wistful, undoubtedly missing Phil.

"The bathroom is through that door," he said, nodding toward one side of the room. "Let's head back downstairs."

"Any special instructions for the bathroom?" she asked.

"Just keep it clean."

They started down the stairs. "How often do you want the upstairs cleaned?"

"The same as the boys' bedrooms—once a week. Mrs. Meadows usually did them all on the same day, but that's up to you."

Autumn decided she'd do that, too. Keeping the rest of the house clean, plus all the cooking… She visualized a life of never-ending chores and silently thanked Judge Niemeyer for making her stay here only sixty days.

"You and your ex must've just broken up," Cody said.

"A few weeks ago."

"I'm sorry."

"Don't be." She didn't hide her anger. "Turns out the rat was already married to someone else."

"That sucks."

"Yep."

The grandfather clock at the foot of the stairs chimed twice. Was it already two o'clock? Dinner was just around the corner. How would she ever manage to prepare enough food for Cody and four teenage boys, let alone serve an edible meal?

She bit her lip. "I'll bet the boys eat a lot."

"Teenagers always do. We get our own breakfasts, so you'll only have to worry about lunch and dinner. Did Judge mention that you get weekends off?"

Autumn was so anxious about dinner that she barely managed a nod.

"You have nothing to worry about," Cody said, as if he'd read her mind. "Like I said earlier, we're easy. We don't expect gourmet meals, just plenty of food."

And a good thing that was, as her idea of gourmet was an upscale frozen dinner. "Judge Niemeyer mentioned an apartment for me."

"It's off an alcove behind the kitchen. Follow me, and this time I'll carry that suitcase."

It was more an order than an offer. Cody disappeared into the foyer and retrieved her bag.

As they traveled down another hall, he pointed out the powder and dining rooms. After a brief stop at the utility room, where he pointed out the washer and dryer and the small pantry stocked with the usual cleaning supplies, he led her to the kitchen.

Gleaming blue-and-white tile counters, pots and pans hanging from a rack above a stainless-steel gas range, a shelf jammed with cookbooks—even though Autumn didn't cook, this was a kitchen straight out of her fantasies. Alongside the usual toaster, coffeemaker and mixer were several unfamiliar appliances she didn't know the names of, let alone have a clue how to operate.

Fresh worry churned in her stomach. "Did Phil and Sylvia have kids?" she asked, noting the big, round dining table in the center of the room.

"They wanted them, and designed the house for a big family. When they learned that wasn't to be, they took in foster kids. In all, they raised over a dozen boys here."

Autumn could only imagine what that must've been like. "All at once?"

Cody shook his head. "Usually four at a time."

"Like you're doing now."

He nodded. "By the time I came along, Sylvia had passed away, and all the boys she and Phil had fostered were grown and scattered across the country. Phil hadn't planned on fostering any more kids, but then I showed up. I was his last."

"Did he keep in contact with any of them?"

"Every one. They all visited when he got sick, with their wives and kids."

"That must've made him happy," Autumn said.

"It did. They came back for his funeral, too. They're good men."

But Cody had done much more than the others. "Selling your company to move back and take care of Phil—that's above and beyond." Filled with new respect and admiration for him, she shook her head.

He shrugged. "It was the least I could do. The man saved my life. And it wasn't as if I took care of him by myself. He hired round-the-clock nurses for that."

"I still can't believe I never knew any of this," Autumn said.

"There's probably a lot I don't know about you, either," Cody said, his expression veiled.

She wondered what he was thinking. Her past was pretty much an open book, and not nearly as interesting as his. If he had questions, she'd answer them. She thought he might, but then he glanced at his watch and his eyes widened. "It's after two already. I need to get out there with my crew."

He pointed out the schedule attached to the refrigerator door, listing each boy's daily chores.

"We rotate the jobs," Cody said. "You'll see that today, Noah and Justin are on dinner cleanup, with Ty and Eric on garden duty. Tomorrow, they switch. They also keep the barn clean and help wherever I need them to. By the way, once you put dinner on the table, you're done for the day. Evenings are yours to spend any way you want."

That sounded great, but she wondered what she would do to pass the time. Being stuck out here on the ranch without a car didn't have a lot to offer nightlifewise. But then, neither did the town of Saddlers Prairie.

"Your apartment is this way." Cody stepped into an alcove behind the kitchen and opened the door. He followed Autumn inside and set her suitcase down. He practically filled the compact living room.

The apartment smelled faintly of fresh paint and disinfectant, and included a bedroom, living room, kitchenette and bathroom. The entire space was about the size of Cody's bedroom, but as long as it was clean and private, it was fine with Autumn.

"It's small," he said. "Feel free to use the house kitchen and anything in it. Same goes for the washer and dryer."

"Thanks."

"This is yours." He dug into his hip pocket and handed her a key. The metal was warm from his body. "If you lose it, I have a spare.

"We eat at six, which gives you some time to settle in before you get started on dinner. There are potatoes, rice and noodles in the pantry, along with everything you need for cookies or brownies."

"You want me to make dessert, too?" Autumn cringed at the panicky squeak in her voice.

"If you have time. Chocolate chip cookies are easy, and a favorite with everyone. Do you have any other questions?"

Tons, such as how exactly did one make chocolate chip cookies? Not about to let on how little she knew, Autumn swallowed. "What if I need groceries?"

"We should be fine for a few days, but you're welcome to borrow one of the Jeeps and pick up what you need. Put the bill on my account."

Autumn hated depending on others for a ride, especially her new boss, but as of Friday afternoon, she didn't have much choice. "I don't own a car," she said, "and I've decided not to drive for a while."

"Because of a few speeding tickets? You're kidding, right?"

"There've been a couple of fender benders, too." She wasn't going to tell him the humiliating rest of the story, but if she wanted to prove she was a responsible person, she had to be honest. "And, um, I lost my insurance." According to the auto insurance company, this latest ticket had been the deciding factor. Apparently one too many infractions made her a bad risk.

She didn't realize she was chewing her bottom lip until Cody stared at her mouth. She quickly stopped.

"This is a busy time of year." He scrubbed the back of his neck. "Tomorrow we start vaccinating and sorting our cattle. It's a morning-till-night process that takes several days. We'll have to wait until Thursday, after breakfast."

Three whole days from now. Would she even *have* a job then? For all she knew, Cody would fire her for her not knowing how to cook. "Thursday's good," she said.

"I'll leave you to it, then. I'll be in the far west pasture, but if you need anything, you can text or call me."

He shut the door behind him. Autumn waited a few seconds before returning to the kitchen, mentally crossing her fingers that she'd find a basic cookbook that explained everything she needed to know.

SEVERAL HOURS LATER, Autumn frowned at the cookie sheets she'd pulled from the oven. Not one of the thirty-six cookies looked right. Each one was as flat as a tortilla and several of them had run together. The edges were black and the middles as gooey-looking as unbaked dough.

Unable to find a beginner cookbook on the shelf, she'd resorted to the recipe on the back of the chocolate chip package. She'd thought she'd followed the directions, but apparently she'd missed something. Well, she wasn't the smartest person around.

Maybe they tasted better than they looked. Wrinkling her nose at the awful burned smell filling the kitchen, Autumn attempted to pry a cookie loose from the tray. The stubborn thing wouldn't budge.

Finally, she used a spoon to scoop a tiny bite from the middle of one cookie. Aside from the charred taste, which somehow permeated even the uncooked center, it was way too salty and not nearly sweet enough.

Grimacing, she chased away the terrible taste with a glass of water.

She needed to start over and try again. The trouble was, at nearly five o'clock—where had the last two hours gone?—there simply wasn't time. Cody and the boys expected dinner at six, and she needed to start the meal right away. Just as soon as she somehow got rid of the bad smell in here.

The fan over the stove would help. But although the motor whirred noisily, the odor remained. She glanced at the back door. Given the record heat outside and the cost of air-conditioning, she wasn't about to open it or the windows. In the powder room, she found a can of air freshener, but the cloying, flowery scent only added to the unpleasant aroma.

With a heavy sigh she acknowledged that she was completely out of her league here. How would she ever last sixty days?

Certain Cody would fire her and she'd wind up in jail after all, Autumn bowed her shoulders. Tears filled her eyes, and for a moment, the world blurred.

But crying would get her nowhere. "Pull it together, Autumn," she muttered, squaring her shoulders.

She *had* to make this work, and darn it, she would. No one needed to know about this little fiasco. Despite the heat, she opened and closed the back door several times, fanning enough hot, dry air into the room to dilute the smell.

Now, what to do with the cookie sheets? She was contemplating stashing them in her room, then burying them in the yard after dark, when she heard the boys' voices in the utility room. She barely had time to shove the sheets back into the oven before Ty and Eric padded into the room in their socks, toting a basket of produce between them.

Ty sniffed and made a face. "What's that smell?"

"It's nothing to worry about." Eager to change the subject, she raised her eyebrows at the basket. "Is that from the garden?"

"Yep," he said, as he and Eric dumped the contents onto the counter.

There were more fresh vegetables than Autumn had ever seen outside of a supermarket. "Am I supposed to use all this for dinner?"

Eric shrugged. "If you want."

"Okay." Canned or frozen vegetables were one thing, but fresh? And so many. Anxiety filled her anew. "I can't believe you boys *grew* all this," she said, shaking her head in wonder.

Ty and Eric straightened with pride.

"We dug the garden, too," Eric said. "Noah and Justin helped."

Ty nodded. "When we got here, the front yard was all grass. Cody showed us how to rototill the ground and mix in old manure to make the soil richer. Manure." He scrunched up his face. "That stuff stinks even worse than this kitchen right now."

"Smells like something burned in here." Eric gave a skeptical snort. "Do you even know how to cook?"

"Of course I do," Autumn said.

Cody said they liked simple food. She'd use the ground beef to make meat loaf, she decided. She'd watched Emilio, Barb's husband and the chef at Barb's Café, make the dish countless times. There wasn't much to it but hamburger and chopped onion. How difficult could it be?

Far easier than making cookies. She'd boil the green

beans the same way she cooked the frozen kind, make a salad from the lettuce and tomatoes, and fix instant white rice. A simple meal sure to please everyone.

"As a matter of fact, I need to start cooking right now," she said. "Thanks for the vegetables."

After the boys thumped down the hall toward the great room, she set to work. With any luck, the savory aroma of baking meat loaf would soon drown out the less pleasant odors.

Chapter Four

A few minutes before six, Cody stepped into the utility room and traded his socks and dirty boots for flip-flops. He washed his face and hands at the sink. After several hours of hard work, he was ravenous enough to eat just about anything. Even so, the smells drifting from the kitchen didn't exactly make his mouth water.

Having already cleaned themselves up, Ty, Eric, Justin and Noah greeted him with unhappy expressions.

"Whatever she's cooking in there stinks," Noah said.

"It's even worse now than when Eric and I brought in the vegetables earlier." Ty grimaced.

"Let's give her a chance," Cody said, although right now, he didn't have much faith, either.

They headed warily into the kitchen, where Autumn was placing steaming bowls and platters on the lazy Susan in the center of the table.

A smudge streaked her cheek, and a big grease stain was splattered across her top. She wore the same hard, don't-mess-with-me expression Cody remembered from her waitressing days.

Yet with her hair pulled into a tight ponytail, exposing her delicate neck, she also seemed vulnerable. A contradiction that for reasons Cody couldn't explain made her extremely appealing.

His stomach rumbled ominously.

"Why don't you join us?" he asked.

Judging by the way her chin lifted, she'd caught the guarded looks the boys exchanged. "That's okay," she said, pulling the ponytail still tighter.

Wanting to put her at ease, Cody smiled. "We insist. This will give us all a chance to get to know each other better. Justin, please set another place."

As the boy complied, Cody gestured at the empty seat. After a brief hesitation, Autumn sat, perching stiffly on her chair.

Once everyone was settled, he spun the lazy Susan so that the meat platter stopped in front of her. He recognized that it was ground beef, but wasn't sure what she'd done to it.

Autumn helped herself to a tiny spoonful. She didn't take much of the beans or rice, either. Either she ate like a bird or she didn't think much of her own cooking.

Cody wasn't sure he would, either, and from the small portions the boys took, they were also leery.

"Where are the biscuits?" Ty asked.

"Was I supposed to make *biscuits?*" Autumn bit her lip. "I didn't know."

"No worries—you didn't have enough time," Cody reassured her.

"Probably woulda ruined them anyway," Eric muttered under his breath. He pushed his chair back and stood.

"Where are you going?" Cody asked.

"To get some bread."

While Eric grabbed the bread and brought it to the table, Noah eyed the glob of meat on his plate. "What is this stuff?"

"Meat loaf," Autumn said.

Ty snickered. "Looks like a big old cow patty to me."

Cody agreed, but he gave the boy a stern look. "That's enough."

"This rice is chewy," Noah lamented.

Too chewy for Cody's tastes, but he managed to swallow a mouthful. Anyone could see Autumn felt badly about the meal, and he wasn't about to make her feel any worse.

She shifted in her seat. "I… It was in a canister without any cooking instructions, so I had to guess."

"You guessed wro—" Ty said, before Cody silenced him with an expression.

"The salad's pretty good." Cody decided to skip the green beans, which still had the ends on them and looked wrinkled and dull.

Justin silently slathered three slices of bread with butter. In short time, he'd devoured them.

After following suit, Eric glared at Autumn. "You can't cook."

She ducked her head and hastily wiped her eyes.

"Aw, come on, you're not bawling, are you?" Eric said, looking stricken.

Cody was right there with him. He never knew what to do with a crying woman. They made him nervous.

She jerked up straight. "Of course not," she replied a touch too brightly.

For some unknown reason, her brave smile touched Cody. "You didn't really have time to get settled and put a meal together tonight, and I shouldn't have expected you to," he said.

"Someone with more experience would've been able to do both. You're right, Eric, I *can't* cook. My mom never did, and I never learned how, but that's no excuse. I should've told you up front, Cody."

Her lower lip quivered, but to his relief, she held herself together. "I'm sorry about dinner. If you want to—" she broke off, swallowed "—to fire me, I understand."

That last part caught him—caught them all—off guard. The room went silent, the boys fixing their gazes on their plates. Whether or not Autumn could cook, they needed her to stay.

"Firing you hasn't even crossed my mind," Cody said.

She released a shaky breath and nodded. "I'll learn how, I promise."

"That's all we ask."

After another loaded silence, she cleared her throat. "Could I have some of that bread?"

Justin passed her what was left of the loaf.

"Anyone besides me want peanut butter on that?" Cody asked, already on his feet.

All the boys did.

"Bring the jelly, too," Ty said.

Having worked hard this afternoon, they were all running on empty, and Cody grabbed a second loaf of bread from the freezer.

After downing a couple sandwiches and a generous helping of salad, Cody felt better. By the color that had returned to Autumn's cheeks, so did she.

"You're welcome to use Sylvia Covey's recipe box and any of the cookbooks," he said, gesturing at the crowded bookshelf near the pantry.

"I looked through some of the books for a chocolate chip cookie recipe, but I couldn't find one I liked, so I used the recipe on the package." Autumn wrinkled her nose. "You don't want to know how those turned out."

"I guess we won't be having dessert tonight," Noah grumbled. "Too bad we're out of ice-cream sandwiches."

Everyone looked dejected.

"There's a stash of candy bars in the pantry that I was

saving for a treat," Cody said. "When we finish eating, I'll break them out."

"That's a relief." Autumn swiped at her brow, and Noah actually cracked a smile.

Ty was a different story. His face a mask of suspicion, he stared at her through narrowed eyes. "We hear you're only here for sixty days—like we're your jail sentence or something. What gives?"

She glanced at Cody in surprise.

"I told them it was up to you to explain," he said. "But only if and when you want to."

Autumn shrugged. "There's no point in hiding the truth. I've racked up a few traffic tickets—who am I kidding, a *lot* of tickets. They're, um, past due, and need to be paid, but at the moment, I don't have the money. Judge Niemeyer offered me a deal. If I perform sixty days of what he calls community service here at Hope Ranch, he'll forgive my debt."

"Community service—what's that?" Noah asked, with no trace of that smile now.

"It means we're some bozo charity project." Stony-faced, Ty crossed his arms.

"It's not really community service, and I don't know why the judge called it that, because I'm getting paid," Autumn said.

Ty didn't appear to hear her. He scraped his chair back and started to rise.

"Sit back down," Cody ordered. "We're not through eating."

"*I'm* through," he muttered, yet he sat. "I'm nobody's charity case."

Autumn had accused Cody of once treating her exactly the same, which made him wonder—did the boys feel he was doing the same thing with them? Something to mull over later.

She regarded Ty with a gentle expression new to Cody. "Believe me, Ty," she said, "I understand exactly how you feel."

"Bullsh—"

"Ty," Cody interrupted sternly.

The boy's mouth slammed shut.

Eric crossed his arms. "Were you ever a foster kid?"

She shook her head.

"Then where do you get off claimin' you know how Ty feels? You don't know nothin'."

Autumn flinched at his harsh tone. "You're right, but I *have* been on the other side of charity. My mom got pregnant with me when she was sixteen. By the time I was born, my dad was long gone. I met him twice— once when I was three, and once just before I turned five. That was the day he let me know he wanted nothing to do with me."

Cody hadn't known that about her. So, she did know about rejection.

"He refused to pay child support," she went on. "My mom took him to court over it, but he disappeared. Since she didn't work, we lived on welfare. Everyone knew how poor we were. I used to hate when people who thought they were better than me gave me handouts. I was so resentful that whenever anyone was nice to me, I assumed that they acted out of pity. Sometimes they were just being decent."

She bit her lip and glanced at Cody, and he understood that she was apologizing for thinking him a snob. In silent acknowledgment, he dipped his head.

Ty's gaze darted between him and Autumn, as if he was trying to puzzle out what was going on. Eric looked equally curious, his eyebrows raised a fraction. Justin shook his head—who knew why—and Noah leaned forward and frowned.

"Where's your mom now?" he asked.

"She lives on the far side of town, but at the moment, she and her current boyfriend are touring the rodeo circuit. He's a saddle bronc rider. Heather and I see each other from time to time, but we're not close."

"Does she do drugs and alcohol?" Justin asked.

It was the first time Justin had asked a question since he'd arrived at the ranch, and Cody hid his surprise.

Autumn shook her head. "She drinks when she goes out, but she's not a drunk. She's had a few boyfriends with addiction problems, though."

The boys seemed to hang on to Autumn's every word. She'd just shared a very personal part of her life that wasn't so different from their own. Judging by their open expressions, they respected her for her candor.

As did Cody. She was so different from the woman he'd thought she was.

"Now I have a question for all of you," she said. "Tell me about Mrs. Meadows."

That broke the spell. The boys glanced uneasily at Cody.

"She was the housekeeper here for over twenty years," he said.

"If she stayed that long, she must have enjoyed the job. Did she leave when Phil died?"

"She stayed on for a while after." Unsure what exactly to say, Cody settled for the bare bones. "Then she decided to retire."

"*That's* what she called it?" Noah gave a hollow laugh.

"She didn't like us, so she up and quit. Mrs. Clinton wasn't any better," Eric added, curling his lip.

"Hey, you weren't exactly easy on either of them," Cody said.

"Because we didn't like *those* old bit—ladies."

"Well, *I* like you, even if you are a tough crowd." Autumn smiled, but none of the boys did.

"You don't even know us." Ty sneered.

"That's true. You don't know me, either, but if you give me a chance, I'll give you a chance."

She'd sold Cody—at least for tonight. God only knew what tomorrow would bring.

The boys seemed uncertain what to think. Eric, Noah and Justin looked to Ty, who blew out a loud breath.

"We're stuck with you for the next sixty days," he grumbled, sounding as if he'd rather have a root canal than deal with her. "May as well."

"Who wants to wash the pots and pans?" Autumn asked Noah and Justin after Ty, Eric and Cody left the kitchen for the great room.

Both boys frowned.

"You're not supposed to hang around after dinner," Noah said. "You get the evening off."

In other words, *go away.* After her nerve-racking day, Autumn was exhausted. She should've jumped at the chance to put her feet up and relax, but she wasn't ready for solitude just yet. "I'd rather help you guys."

"You don't think we can do it." Noah made a spitting noise, as if expelling a bad taste from his mouth.

Justin shook his head and kicked the tile with his foot.

"It's not that. What if I said I actually enjoy cleaning the kitchen after a meal?"

Noah snorted.

"I mean it. Cleaning makes me feel good. It always has. I'd really like to help."

"Whatever," he mumbled. "It's my turn to wash the dishes. Justin loads the dishwasher and sweeps up. There isn't much else for you to do." His voice cracked and his face reddened.

Autumn pretended not to notice. "You haven't seen those cookie sheets." When she'd preheated the oven for the meat loaf earlier, she'd forgotten having stashed them in the oven. The cookies had burned into a charred mess.

She opened the back door, where she'd stowed the baking sheets after filling them with ammonia and wrapping them in plastic trash bags—a trick she'd learned from a dishwasher at Barb's.

She set them carefully on the counter, and the disbelief on the boys' faces was priceless. She bit back a smile. "I don't think either of you want to clean these."

"Nope," Noah said. "Why don't you just throw them out?"

Justin nodded. "Cody has plenty of money. He'll buy new ones."

"Why should he, when all they need is a good scrubbing? I'll clean them after you finish the other dishes. For now, I'll just grab a sponge and wipe off the kitchen table."

Noah and Justin exchanged looks, then Noah gave a resigned sigh. "You want an apron?"

Glancing at her stained, food-spattered tunic top and jeans, Autumn laughed. "It's a little late for that." She'd meant to coax out a smile, but the boys remained tense, as if her company was a real trial for them.

"If you change your mind, they're in the bottom drawer," Noah said.

Autumn ignored Justin's why-are-you-kissing-up-to-her look. "Thanks, Noah. Cody forgot to tell me that. I'll definitely wear one tomorrow."

The boy's scowl loosened, as if she'd said exactly what he needed to hear. As defensive and unfriendly as he was, underneath he seemed eager to please, and Autumn sensed that in time he might even grow to like her.

Justin was a different story. Besides being painfully thin, he had a hard-edged demeanor that broke her heart. He probably wasn't nearly as tough as he wanted to appear.

She understood. How many times had she worn the same flinty-eyed, back-off look? Now and then she still did. She didn't trust anyone easily, either—including her own self. Not after all the bad choices she'd made and was still making.

But if she wanted to survive this job for sixty days, she'd best try to win him over.

"Do you ever wear aprons?" she asked, addressing Justin.

He shook his head and turned on the faucet, deterring further conversation. With three of them pitching in, the room was tidy in no time.

"Thank you both for putting the kitchen back in order," Autumn said. "And for letting me help."

Noah gave a jerky nod, Justin grunted and they lumbered away without a backward glance, no doubt to relax in front of the tube with the others.

Autumn filled the sink with hot, soapy water and immersed the cookies sheets. The ammonia soak had helped, and some of the char had come off. In the breaks between bouts of furious scrubbing and rinsing, she heard sounds from the TV and sporadic bursts of laughter from Cody and the boys. They had their problems, but at the moment, they sounded like a family.

Joining them at the dinner table had been unexpected and slightly uncomfortable, and she certainly hadn't anticipated an invitation to watch TV with them. She told herself she was more comfortable with her own company, yet on the heels of the thought, a wave of loneliness broadsided her.

She'd always longed to be part of a real family. When Teddy had proposed and offered to build her a house with enough bedrooms for several kids, she'd thought her dreams had at last come true, that she'd finally found someone she could depend on. A man who wanted the same things she did—a life together and a baby or two. Ha.

The funny part was she'd never really loved him. Instead, she'd fallen in love with the *idea* of love.

The cookie sheets looked almost as good as before. Autumn rinsed and dried them, then put them away. Thanks to Facebook and updates from Sherry, she knew that some of their former high school classmates had moved away. Just about everyone was either engaged, married or divorced. Most had kids or were planning to start families. Sherry was none of the above, but she did have a serious boyfriend who she expected would eventually propose. Without a boyfriend or children, Autumn felt like the odd person out. But that was nothing new.

Sometimes she wondered if she'd ever have the family or live the kind of life she'd once dreamed of. Without more schooling, and only herself to depend on, her odds of earning enough for financial security weren't good.

If she had the brains, she'd go to college, get an education and make something of herself—another useless dream. She'd never done well in school.

With a sigh, she plunked down on a kitchen chair and pondered how to spend the rest of her evening. It was way too early to go to bed, and she didn't feel like unpacking just yet, or vegging in front of the small TV in her living room. She'd bought several magazines and a paperback book at Spenser's, but she wasn't in the mood for reading, either.

Her wandering gaze lit on the shelf of cookbooks. Now was the perfect time to cull through recipes and make a grocery list, so that when Cody took her to town, she'd know what to buy.

Feeling better now that she had something to do, Autumn stood and headed for the cookbooks.

FROM HIS PLACE on the sofa, Cody greeted Noah and Justin as they sauntered into the great room after cleaning up in the kitchen. Noah seemed different, his footsteps lighter, his narrow shoulders straighter.

"Autumn hung around and helped us," he announced in wonder.

That she'd helped when she didn't have to was surprising enough, but what impressed Cody even more was the subtle change in Noah. Already he seemed taken with the new housekeeper.

Ty gave him a disgusted look. "You like her."

"Fool," Eric said.

Wearing a mock smile, Justin ducked his head.

"Shut up." Noah glared at them all. "She's better than the other housekeepers and you know it."

"But she's a lousy cook," Ty retorted, his eyes on the television.

"You heard what she said—she's gonna learn how."

"You really believe that?" Eric shook his head. "Who wants to bet on how long she lasts?"

"She'll make it the whole sixty days," Noah said with certainty.

"You—"

"Shh," Cody said. "I can't hear the program."

Not that he cared, but the comment drew the boys' attention to the TV sitcom.

Deep in thought, Cody had no idea what happened on the screen. Autumn had been here less than half a day and already was making an impact. For the boys' sake, he hoped Noah was right and she stayed. Otherwise, they were bound to be hurt. None of them needed one more adult letting them down. Autumn should understand that, and now seemed a good time to explain.

He stretched. "Think I'll head into the kitchen and see what she's up to in there."

He didn't miss the looks the boys exchanged.

"What about the show?" Ty asked.

"Fill me in later."

"Treat her nice," Noah said, as Cody headed for the hallway.

Chapter Five

Ready to plan half a dozen meals, and armed with a pen and notebook so that she could make the grocery list, Autumn sat down at the kitchen table. Instead of opening one of the cookbooks piled in front of her, she reached for Sylvia Covey's wooden recipe box.

The contents were arranged by category, with handwritten recipes and others clipped from a newspaper attached to index cards. Autumn went straight to the Main Dish tab. Mrs. Covey had listed the ingredients, but her directions were mostly limited to baking temperatures and cooking times. Not a word about how to put it all together. Nothing in the other categories was any more helpful.

Frustrated, Autumn set the box aside and opened a cookbook that had caught her eye for its color photos. To her relief, the book provided actual instructions. Unfortunately, they were complicated, and following them would be a problem. After a few minutes, Autumn threw up her hands. For all she understood, the steps could've been written in gibberish.

The next cookbook she checked proved equally confusing. What was the matter with the publishers? Why did they make everything so hard to figure out?

Maybe the problem was her.

Feelings Autumn thought she'd buried long ago overwhelmed her—that she wasn't as smart as other people, and that maybe, as with everything else in life, she would fail at this, too.

No, she sternly insisted. If she wanted to avoid going to jail and prove that she was responsible, she *had* to succeed at Hope Ranch.

Determined, she opened a third cookbook. This time, instead of puzzling over unfamiliar cooking terms and instructions, and giving up in frustration, she jotted down words to look up.

She was scribbling furiously in the notebook when the door between the kitchen and hallway clicked shut.

Autumn almost jumped out of her skin—and then saw Cody ambling toward her. She'd been so intent on what she was doing that she hadn't heard his footsteps.

"You startled me!" she said.

"So I see." Mouth quirking, he eyed the cookbooks spread over the table. "Looking through recipes?"

"For dinner ideas. I'm working on a grocery list for Thursday."

"Good idea."

He leaned against the counter, casual yet purposeful. Had she done something else wrong? Autumn bit the inside of her cheek.

"I came in here to let you know how important consistency is to the boys," he said. "They need adults in their lives who stick around."

Why was he telling her this? "Of course they do, but I'm only here sixty days. They know that."

He nodded but didn't reply. His expression unreadable, he stroked his chin with his thumb and forefinger multiple times, an action reminding Autumn of Phil.

It took her a moment to realize what Cody meant. "You think I'm going to quit," she said, stung.

"I didn't say that, and I hope you don't," he stated. "I don't want the boys hurt."

Did they know how lucky they were to have a foster dad who genuinely cared about them? Still, Cody had just insulted her. She stiffened. "As I assured Judge Niemeyer the other day, I'm a woman of my word. I promise that I'll be here for the full sixty days."

The judge had accepted her promise at face value. Cody seemed more cautious. "You say that now, but in a day or two you might change your mind." Before she could question him, he nodded at the cookbooks. "Find anything that looks good?"

If he wanted to change the subject, it was fine with her. "I haven't decided yet," she said, not wanting to admit that the cookbooks were way beyond her level of skill.

On the other hand, he already knew she couldn't cook worth beans, so why pretend? "None of Mrs. Covey's recipes come with instructions, and these cookbooks are pretty confusing. I have tons of questions." Autumn scanned her notes. "Do you know how to blanch tomatoes, or what dicing means? What's a ricer? And how exactly do you use a meat thermometer?"

"Beats me," Cody said. "I can use the barbecue, but that's the extent of my cooking skills. What exactly does the recipe say?"

Autumn flipped to the page that mentioned the ricer. Moving to stand behind her, he peered over her shoulder and frowned at the recipe. He wasn't close enough to touch her, but near enough that she smelled the sun and heat of the day, and underneath, his subtle masculine scent. It filled her senses and flirted with her mind, so that she no longer had any idea what the cookbook said.

Suddenly, he leaned down, his head inches above hers. So close she would barely have to raise her hand to touch the fine stubble on his jaw. He seemed focused on the recipe, but Autumn couldn't help wondering whether that was just a ploy, and whether he felt something for her, too.

Was this why he'd shut the door?

If he turned his head a fraction and she angled hers the tiniest little bit toward him, their lips would…

Stop.

She was no longer the gullible, love-starved woman she'd once been. She was strong and independent….

She glanced at him out of the corner of her eyes but his attention was fully on the cookbook. Not on her.

Of course it was. Cody Naylor had a college degree, buckets of money and a successful ranch. He wasn't interested in her.

As if to underline her thoughts, he straightened and stepped back. "These cookbooks are for people with advanced skills," he said. "You need something more basic."

No kidding. She also needed to ground herself firmly in reality and stop fantasizing about a kiss from Cody Naylor. "I didn't see anything like that on the shelf," she said.

"Spenser's probably sells cookbooks for beginners." Cody sat down across the table from her. "We'll check on Thursday. If we don't find what you need, we'll order something online."

Autumn nodded. His short hair was dark and thick, and the sun had tinted his broad forehead and well-defined features. His eyes seemed equally sun-drenched, the irises a deep chocolate color, with multiple gold flecks lightening them to a whiskey-brown.

He caught her staring. Something dark and sensual flared in his eyes before Autumn glanced away.

"A beginner's cookbook is exactly what I need," she managed to say.

Looking at his face was dangerous, so she glanced at his fingers. They were large and clean. One blunt nail was black, no doubt from a ranching mishap, and there were blisters in the crook of his thumb. His hands screamed hard, manual labor, yet also skillfully navigated a cell phone and computer.

Her body tingled as if those callused fingers had brushed across her skin. *What's the matter with me?*

Autumn reached for the recipe box and pretended to shuffle through it. "Shouldn't you be in the great room with the boys?" she asked, praying Cody didn't guess her feelings.

"They're probably relieved to have some time without me. I wanted to talk with you privately about what happened at dinner."

So, *this* was why he'd shut the door. Hadn't they discussed her awful cooking enough for one night? Her shoulders stiffened. "I said I was sorry about dinner."

"And I said I'm not at all worried. You're a smart woman. Once you get your hands on the right cookbook, you'll figure out what you need to know."

He thought she was smart? Warmth flooded her, and she was sure she must be glowing.

Until she realized that Cody knew nothing about her intelligence or lack thereof. He was simply being nice. Or maybe she was better at hiding her limited brain power than she thought.

"Autumn?" He cocked his head and furrowed his brow, as if trying to figure out what she was thinking.

"You said something about what happened at dinner?" she prompted.

Cody nodded. "Your interactions with the boys." Even

though the door was shut, he spoke in a low voice that wouldn't carry far.

She'd screwed that up, too? Great, he was going to chew her out, after all. Resisting the urge to gnaw her thumbnail, she effected an unconcerned expression. "You didn't give me any direction, Cody. Tell me what you expect, and I'll do my best to follow through."

"You don't need any instructions from me, Autumn. You handled the boys beautifully."

She had? Autumn frowned.

"Some of the things you said reminded me so much of Phil, it almost felt like he was talking through you," Cody went on. "What you told Ty when he got defensive and said he was nobody's charity case… And Eric, when he claimed the housekeepers disliked him and the other boys. You got Noah to smile, and Justin… That kid soaked up your every word. How the heck did you do that?"

Cody looked awed, which made Autumn even more uncomfortable. She pulled the elastic out of her hair and made a fresh ponytail. "I don't know. I just bumbled along until something worked."

"Your so-called bumbling is amazing. Telling the boys about your father and your mom, that you grew up on welfare… *I* didn't even know about that."

"It's not something I'm proud of, and I'd appreciate if you'd keep it to yourself outside the house. But tonight…" Pausing, Autumn searched for the right words. "I thought the boys would be more accepting of me if they understood that they aren't the only ones who've suffered through hard times."

"You thought right. You were respectful toward them, and the way you addressed their concerns showed that you really heard them. I suspect few adults in their lives have been as genuine or candid as you."

Autumn soaked up the praise. Her heart began to open, but she quickly forced it shut. She was past naively giving her heart when a man told her what she wanted to hear.

"Their lives have been filled with lies and evasions," Cody continued. "They've become BS detector experts, and when someone tells the truth, they appreciate it—even though they may not let on."

Having a mother like hers, Autumn also knew about lies and evasions. Heather had never been exactly straightforward about her various boyfriends, always painting them as nicer and more successful than they really were. She'd lied about other things, as well. Promising to come to an evening school program, then not showing up because of some random excuse. Staying out all night and pretending she'd slept at a girlfriend's house, when she'd really gone home with some guy she'd met in a bar.

You'd think that after living with that the first sixteen years of her life, Autumn would be great at spotting liars, but she wasn't. Every one of her boyfriends had lied about one thing or another, Teddy being the worst yet.

The sad truth was Autumn had never been involved with a truly honest man. Which was why she was through with men until she honed her own BS meter.

"I've been lied to myself," she said.

"Same here, and like you, I shared my own sorry story with the boys. But I never hit it off with them the way you did tonight."

"I wouldn't exactly say we hit it off."

"You're sure headed in that direction. It hasn't been like that with me."

"Are you kidding?" Autumn gave a disbelieving laugh. "Those boys worship you."

"Hardly. I'm tough, but fair, and they respect that. But you… You're pretty, and a natural with teenage boys."

Cody thought she was pretty. But Autumn had heard that often enough that the words barely registered. "You're sweet to say so."

"I'm not trying to be sweet." He rested his forearms on the table and gave her a level look. "When Justin asked that question about your mother… In the four months since he arrived here, that kid has never asked a single question, not of me or, as far as I know, of Ty, Eric or Noah. Tonight was a first for him, and you're damn straight, I'm impressed."

Unnerved by the compliment, which was much harder to accept than the usual stuff men handed her about her looks, Autumn returned to the subject that had negatively impressed Cody. "But my cooking is awful."

"And you'll get better at it. Please, God, get better or we'll all starve."

His teasing smile coaxed out her own, and something shifted between them. The air thickened, wrapping them in intimacy, so that sitting together, talking in low voices almost felt like the end of a good first date.

But this was no date. She was the hired help and Cody was her boss.

She glanced at the digital clock over the stove. "It's already nine-thirty, and I still need to unpack. Good night." She scooped up the recipe box and several cookbooks, and carried them to the shelf.

Cody rose, too, and gathered up the rest.

As Autumn turned toward the alcove, he stopped her with a touch, a light graze of his fingertips against her forearm. Warmth traveled up her arm.

Their gazes met before Cody's eyes dropped to her lips. Then she knew: he wanted to kiss her.

She wasn't going to let that happen, she reminded herself, even while every nerve in her body strained toward him.

Abruptly, he dropped his hand and stepped back, looking as stunned as Autumn felt.

WHILE CODY PULLED HIMSELF together, Autumn snatched her notebook from the table and clutched it to her chest. As if the flimsy spiral thing could protect her from the heat swirling between them….

He wanted badly to kiss her. How could he not? Every word she spoke drew his attention to her lush, pink, unpainted lips. Her skin had felt smooth, a whisper of silk against his rough fingers. And her startled expression, her eyes registering her own attraction to him… It was difficult enough to resist that.

But what drew him even more was her innate ability to relate to the damaged boys in his care—that and her determination to master a few cooking skills.

Still, she was his housekeeper, and she was here only because the judge had ordered it. If Cody wanted her to stay the full sixty days, and he did, he'd best—

"You wanted to say something else?" she asked, nervously clicking her ballpoint pen.

He cleared his throat. "It may seem as if the boys are starting to accept you, but you're not home free," he warned. "They all have trust issues…"

She slid the pen into the notebook's spiral binding. "Justin most of all. Whatever happened in his past has really scarred him," she said, surprising Cody yet again with her insights.

She was dead-on, but without the boy's permission,

Cody wasn't free to disclose any confidential information about his background. "That's Justin's story to share," he said. "If you earn his trust, he just might. The same goes for the other boys."

"I want them to trust me, but I know it won't be easy," she said. "Do you have any advice for me?"

Cody shared what Phil had told him when they'd discussed Cody's idea for Hope Ranch. "No matter what happens, stay in the game. By that I mean operate with a firm, but caring hand. Follow through on your word, and expect them to test you often, in ways you can't even imagine."

"Test?" Autumn's forehead puckered. "What do you mean by that?"

"Each of the boys is a chronic runaway. Things get rough and they run. Over the past few years, not one of them stayed home for more than a few weeks at a time. That's the main reason they wound up with me in Saddlers Prairie—with limited traffic heading out of town, and the nearest bus depot a good twenty-five miles away, taking off isn't so easy."

"You chose a great location for Hope Ranch," Autumn said.

"Credit Phil and Sylvia for that. Anyway, about a week after Ty arrived, almost four months ago, he decided he hated being here. He hot-wired Mrs. Meadows's car."

Autumn covered her mouth with her fingers. "Did he get very far?"

Cody let out a humorless laugh. "The kid knows how to get a motor running, but he doesn't know how to drive."

"Let me guess. He totaled the car."

"Not quite, but in his hurry to leave, he rammed the corner of the barn. Destroyed the right front end of the vehicle and caused a fair amount of damage to the building."

"That sounds worse than any of my fender benders. What did Mrs. Meadows do?"

"Gave her two weeks' notice. She failed Ty's trust test."

"I can't say that I blame her. What *should* she have done?"

"Chewed him out, withheld dessert, forced him to pay her back by giving him extra chores—anything except quit on him."

Autumn looked pensive, then slowly nodded. "That makes sense."

"Mrs. Meadows wanted to retire after Phil died. She only stayed on because I asked. But those boys drained her."

"What do you do with your cars? Do you keep them locked up? And what about the horses? Any of the boys could ride away."

Cody shook his head. "They're new to riding, and not that comfortable in the saddle. Besides, this ranch is their last chance. I didn't report Ty for what he did, but he knows that if he attempts to run again, I will. He'll be locked up in juvenile detention for a while. Noah, Eric and Justin are pretty much in the same boat. Even so, they'll test you, both individually and as a group, so stay alert."

"I will. Thanks for the warning." Though the kitchen felt anything but cold to Cody, Autumn chafed her arms.

He itched to run his hands over those arms and warm her up. "They're not a danger to themselves or others," he said, curling his fingers at his sides. "If they were, they wouldn't be here."

"That's a relief."

Annoyed with his unwanted attraction to her, he checked his watch. "I should get back to them."

He pivoted away and left the room.

Chapter Six

"Where's Autumn?" Noah asked, as he helped himself to the breakfast sandwich Cody had fixed Thursday morning. "She was here yesterday morning and the day before."

Wondering the same thing himself, Cody washed down his food with coffee before replying. "Technically, she doesn't have to be here during breakfast. I'm driving her to Spenser's in a little while, and I'll bet she's either getting ready to go, or eating in her own kitchen."

"How do you know she didn't take off in the middle of the night?" the boy persisted, his anxious expression adding years to his young face.

Ty's bark sounded like a laugh gone wrong. "Wouldn't be the first time the housekeeper skipped out on us."

"If you hadn't acted like a total douche again last night at dinner—"

"Because I still don't like the crap she serves? I'm not a butt kisser like you."

"Take that back or—"

"Will you two ease up?" Cody sent the two angry boys warning looks. "She's still here. I'd stake my right arm on that."

Since Autumn's arrival, she'd joined them nightly at the dinner table. Her meals were still pretty bad, but she was trying. After that first night, Cody had avoided her unless one of the boys was around, his unwanted attraction to her carefully under wraps, where it would stay. "Hopefully, we'll find a cookbook today to help with the food situation," he added.

If he had his way, this would be the first and only time he'd drive her into town. He couldn't spare the time to taxi her around, and intended to convince her to drive herself from now on.

"I'll bet she's still asleep," Eric said. "We hafta get up at six. Autumn should, too."

"You get up then because I need your help around the ranch," Cody reminded him. "Especially with the haying in front of us. The past few days haven't been easy for her. Maybe she's tired."

Cody sure was. He took a long pull of his coffee. He wasn't sleeping well—too restless. It didn't help that in the dark of night, his unfettered thoughts centered on Autumn. Hot, sensual thoughts he had no right to have, and that would only lead to trouble. Frowning, he stood and refilled his coffee.

Ty emptied the last of the milk into his glass and headed for the refrigerator for another gallon. "We only have two of these left," he said when he returned to the table with the jug.

Cody nodded. "We'll pick up more at Spenser's."

After breakfast, the boys loaded their dishes into the dishwasher and chatted eagerly about their ranch chores. They complained about getting up early, but seemed to enjoy tending the cattle and working with the crew.

Cody enjoyed the work, too. Anxious to get the shopping over with, he turned toward Autumn's apartment to remind her that he wanted to leave soon. He was entering the alcove when her door opened.

Yawning, wearing a lime-green tank top that clung to her generous breasts, a short denim skirt and canvas wedge sandals, she looked summery and sexy. As usual, her hair was pulled back into a ponytail. She couldn't be more than five foot five, but in that skirt and those shoes, her legs looked impossibly long. She smelled good, too, like lilacs.

Cody couldn't help gawking at her. And neither could the boys—that was, before their faces took on their usual mistrust.

"You slept in," Ty grumbled.

"Good morning to you, too." Autumn yawned again. "I set the alarm last night but it never went off."

Eric gave her a censuring look. "That's wack."

Refusing to make eye contact with anyone, Justin brushed nonexistent crumbs from his T-shirt. Noah was the only one who looked openly pleased to see her.

"I swear, there's something wrong with it," Autumn said. "Try it yourself if you don't believe me."

"Okay." Ty jerked his chin toward her apartment, and all four boys stalked through the door.

Autumn shot Cody an alarmed look before dashing after them.

Knowing this could be the first big test, Cody followed them into the apartment. Autumn rushed into her tiny kitchen, snatched a dented steel canister from a cabinet and hugged it to her chest, as if she feared someone would steal it.

Ty's face registered shock, which he quickly masked. He crossed his arms rigidly over his chest and narrowed his eyes. "You got weed in there?"

"No," she said adamantly. "I don't use drugs."

"Then why you huggin' that thing like it was yo

baby?" Eric asked from the kitchen doorway, his splayed feet and bent elbows pure gangsta.

"That's none of your business."

Cody sided with Autumn, but was curious as hell. What did she keep in there?

Standing behind Eric, Noah was stony-faced. "Whatever you've got stashed in there, you're scared we'll boost it."

Radiating tension, Justin shoved his hands into his pockets and squinted at the floor.

All the boys displayed defensive, angry poses Cody hadn't seen in weeks.

He stifled a frustrated groan. Any gains Autumn had made with the boys over the past few days had just been obliterated, and by her dismayed expression, she knew it.

"Time to saddle up and get over to the north pasture," he said. "Tell Doug and the rest of the crew that as soon as I get back from Spenser's, I'll join you."

After the boys had disappeared through the door, Autumn set the canister on the counter and buried her face in her hands. "I really screwed that up, didn't I?"

"You could've handled it better," Cody conceded.

"I don't want them going through my stuff."

"That's understandable. I was about to remind them to respect your privacy, but I never got the chance."

"That was one of their tests, wasn't it? I overreacted, and I failed," she said, working her bottom lip like gum.

It was all Cody could do not to pull her into a reassuring hug. "You didn't do anything that can't be fixed."

"You think I can fix this? How?" she asked, her eyes big and round and hopeful.

He got lost in the depths of those eyes. The kitchen didn't leave much room for two people to stand, and he was close enough to see the fine dusting of freckles across her cheeks.

"Tell me how," she repeated.

For a moment he wasn't sure what she meant. He tore his gaze away. "I don't exactly know, but I'll tell you what helps me. The boys know that I care about them, and that I'm here for them no matter what. If you like them and they know it, sooner or later they'll forgive and forget."

"I don't know how to show that I like them."

"Just keep doing what you've already been doing—be honest, be open, be warm."

Autumn nodded. "Should I leave my apartment unlocked?"

"I wouldn't."

Cody heard the grandfather clock chime. They'd best get moving. "If you want coffee and breakfast before we go, better have them now," he said, gesturing toward the door.

Despite this morning's fiasco, Autumn walked with a swing in her step. Her curvy hips swayed seductively, the motion pulling the skirt taut across her round behind.

What with Phil being sick and his subsequent death, then getting Hope Ranch up and going, Cody hadn't been with a woman in close to a year. A certain part of his body tightened and started to rise. He forced his gaze from Autumn's delectable backside.

She found a travel mug in the cabinet, to which she added coffee, milk and sugar. "I'll fix myself a piece of toast and bring it with me."

"Just toast? That won't feed a bird."

"If I get hungry later, I'll fix myself a snack."

While waiting for the bread to toast, she took a sip of her coffee, then closed her eyes and murmured in pleasure. Cody couldn't help imagining her in the throes of passion.

His body hardened. Not wanting her to catch him lusting over her, he turned to the fridge.

"Do you want butter and jam?" His harsh tone earned him a curious look. "On your toast," he added in a friendlier voice.

"Yes, please." Autumn stretched and yawned once more, drawing his attention to her breasts. They would fill a man's hands and then some.

He pinned his eyes on her face, leaned against the counter and crossed his arms. "You're still tired," he said gruffly.

"I really did set the alarm on that clock," she said, misinterpreting his tone. "I have no idea why it didn't work."

"It's old. We'll pick up a new one at Spenser's."

Autumn nodded. "If I'm lucky and find a cookbook that actually makes sense to me, I might choose a recipe from it right there in the store and pick up whatever ingredients I need."

"You're taking this cooking stuff seriously."

"Why wouldn't I?" She looked at him as if he'd suddenly turned orange. "I promised you and the boys. I just hope they aren't too angry to give me a chance."

"Trust me, if you stick with them, they'll get over it. That reminds me—add four gallons of milk to your grocery list."

"Four?"

"The boys like their milk, and I don't have the time to head back into town whenever we run out of something. It'd help if you started driving again."

Autumn spread butter and jelly on her toast, which she set on a paper towel. "Let me grab my purse and we can go." When she returned, she said, "Trust me, Cody, you don't want me driving any of your cars."

"Yeah, I do. I don't have time to chauffeur you around. Stay within the speed limit and you'll be fine."

"I don't know...." She looked unconvinced.

"Tell you what—I'll drive to Spenser's. You drive back, and we'll see how you do."

Autumn sighed. "I'll think about it."

CODY PUT ON his baseball cap and mirrored aviator sunglasses. As soon as Autumn buckled in, he started the truck and drove fast down the driveway, past the vast rolling fields of Hope Ranch. It was obvious that he was in a big hurry to get this outing over with. Hating that she'd inconvenienced him, she vowed to find what she needed in record time.

"How big is the ranch?" she asked in an effort to start a conversation.

"A thousand acres. We've got four hundred head of cattle."

"That's huge."

"Not really, but it's perfect for me."

His satisfied smile spoke volumes. He obviously loved living here. It was where he belonged.

Autumn nibbled her toast and wondered at that. Heather had moved them around town often, and Autumn had never had the chance to grow attached to any place she'd lived.

If she found a real job after leaving the ranch—no, *when* she found a real job—she'd rent a place and stay there for a while. Maybe a cottage with a little yard, where she could grow her own vegetables, like the boys did.

First, though, she needed to make this job work.

Which meant earning their trust. The thought made her lose her appetite, and she gave up on her toast.

"See that hay baler in the far north field?" Cody gestured out the window. "That's where the boys are today."

The sun had been up a scant few hours, but it was already hot and bright, and even wearing sunglasses, Autumn had to squint. She saw horses clustered under a small grove of trees, the only shade in the area. The boys and the crew would be spending the whole day in the sun.

"It's already hotter than an oven," she said, cranking up the air-conditioning. "I hope they don't get heatstroke."

"If they keep their hats on and drink plenty of fluids, they'll be fine." Cody pulled onto the highway, leaving the ranch behind.

"Still, a full day of physical labor seems a lot for teenage boys."

"It is, and they don't usually do that much. But the hay won't keep, and for the next few days we need all the help we can get. Hard work is good for them, and they enjoy earning their own money. They're also learning discipline and how to work with other people. As a bonus, they get to experience the thrill of accomplishment. Those are the kinds of lessons that turned my life around."

"I wish someone had taught me those things when I was a teen," Autumn said.

A sudden flash of light in the distance brought her up straight. "Did you see that?"

Cody nodded. "Dry lightning. It's that time of year. Cross your fingers it doesn't start any fires around here."

When she'd waitressed, she'd often heard ranchers grumbling about lightning fires. "Have you ever had one at the ranch?"

"Unfortunately, yes. The forest service has a supply

of water pumpers they loan out to control and extinguish the fires. They have to be filled from time to time, which is a pain, but they help control the damage."

Cody drove on, pushing the speed limit. The highway was empty, but that didn't mean Sheriff Bennett wasn't hiding someplace with his radar gun.

Keeping a wary eye out for flashing lights, she changed the subject. "The boys mentioned ice-cream sandwiches at dinner that first night. I'm thinking I'll serve those for dessert tonight. That way, they'll know I was listening."

"Good call," Cody said with approval.

Autumn took another sip of her coffee and then posed the question that had been on her mind since she'd arrived here. "You're a wealthy man—you could hire all the help you need at the ranch. Why not just sit back and relax?"

He looked surprised. "I happen to enjoy the work. Besides, sitting around watching other people do the work isn't my thing."

He glanced at her. "You're frowning," he said. "What's wrong with that?"

"Nothing. I just never pictured you as a rancher. Back when I used to wait on you, you were always talking all this high-tech stuff. I assumed that was your passion."

"It was for a while. But when Phil was diagnosed with cancer and I came back here to be with him, I realized how much I missed ranching. It's in my blood."

"Phil was like a father to you, wasn't he?"

"More than my biological father ever was."

Cody swallowed as if he had a big lump in his throat, and Autumn knew he missed Phil.

"You're a lucky man for having known him," she said.

"Don't I know it," Cody agreed, smiling at her.

In what seemed to Autumn like no time at all, Cody pulled into the potholed dirt parking lot shared by Spenser's, Barb's Café, the post office and the few other businesses in downtown Saddlers Prairie. At this hour most people were either ranching or at other jobs, and the lot was all but empty.

The instant she opened the truck door and slid out of her seat, the heat assaulted her and sweat beaded on her upper lip.

Cody pulled off his baseball cap and wiped his forehead. "I'll help with the shopping. That way we can get back sooner."

Autumn felt guiltier than ever for taking him away from his chores. "Great," she said. "You can show me which brands you and the boys prefer. By the way, I think I will drive us back."

He grinned. "That's my girl."

She knew he didn't mean that the way it sounded. She wasn't his girl and never would be. All the same, she liked hearing the words.

Cody grabbed a cart and followed her through the automated doors. In contrast to the bright sunlight, the store interior seemed dark. Autumn pulled off her sunglasses and blinked.

When her eyes adjusted, she saw Connie Volles, a woman roughly Cody's age who worked as a checker, staring at her with a curious expression. She hadn't been working when Autumn had been there the previous weekend, but this was a small town where everyone knew everyone else's business, and she assumed Connie knew about the deal she'd worked out with Judge Niemeyer.

"Hey, Autumn, it's been a while." Connie's gaze slid to Cody. "I don't usually see you in here on a Thursday morning."

"I needed a ride to pick up groceries, and Cody was nice enough to offer," Autumn said. "But he has to get right back to the ranch and we're in a hurry. Where are your cookbooks?"

The clerk's penciled eyebrows lifted slightly, as if she couldn't believe Cody was here with Autumn, or buying her a cookbook.

"She needs something that explains the basics, with easy-to-follow directions," Cody added.

He'd just announced that Autumn was stupid. Heat scalded her cheeks.

"Any cookbooks we have are along the back shelf with the other nonfiction," Connie said.

"Thanks." Without a backward glance at Cody, Autumn strode toward the rear of the store.

"Wait up," he called out, wheeling the cart. "I'm not in *that* big a hurry."

Ignoring his teasing smile, she quickened her pace.

"Autumn. Stop."

She blew out a loud breath and spun toward him. "What?"

"You're upset."

"That's right, I am. I am *not* stupid."

"Stupid?" Cody looked confused. "I never said you were."

"You implied as much when you told Connie I need easy-to-follow instructions."

"Damn, you're sensitive. I was just trying to help."

It was what Eric would call a "wack" excuse.

"We need cheddar cheese and the milk you mentioned," Autumn said. "And ice-cream sandwiches. You get those while I pick out a cookbook." She whirled away from him and continued to the book section.

She found the perfect beginner's manual, with simple

but detailed instructions, and sketches of utensils and equipment. Exactly the kind of book Cody had asked about.

He was right; she *was* sensitive. For the second time this morning she'd overreacted. Now she owed both Cody and the boys apologies.

The day had started out badly and seemed to be only getting worse. Autumn was so discouraged that tears gathered behind her eyes. Refusing to give in to self-pity, she compressed her lips and flipped through the book to the entrée section, where she found several promising dishes.

Learning to cook was one way to show the boys she cared. Earning their trust was another. As daunting as it seemed, Autumn was determined to master both.

From this moment on, Cody wouldn't regret letting her work for him—she'd make sure of that.

Chapter Seven

Opening the cookbook to the recipe she wanted to try, Autumn headed up the closest food aisle in search of ingredients.

She found several of the items she needed. Wishing she had the grocery cart instead of Cody, she filled her arms with them. She was on her way to get a basket when she heard a baby gurgle, followed by a child's pleased giggle. Around the corner of the next aisle, she spotted Jenny Dawson and two young children.

Autumn hadn't seen the other woman in ages. "Hi, Jenny," she called out, hurrying toward her with a genuine smile.

"Autumn!" Jenny's own smile radiated warmth. "I heard you were back. I like your hair—it's longer and a different color."

"This is my natural color."

"Well, it looks great. *You* look great."

"Thanks. It's been a rough few weeks, but I'm okay now," Autumn said. "Don't ever run off with a man you've only known for forty-eight hours." But then, Jenny wouldn't. She was married to her soul mate, the handsome rancher Adam Dawson.

"You remember Abby." Jenny gestured to the little

girl, who'd shot up since Autumn had last seen her. "Do you remember Autumn? She used to wait on us at Barb's."

The redheaded girl flashed her dimples. "You always put extra sprinkles on my ice-cream sundae."

You'd never guess that she hadn't been able to speak until after she'd entered kindergarten at the one-room school where Jenny taught. Autumn grinned. "Good memory, Abby."

The apple-cheeked baby babbled charmingly, and Autumn cooed at him. "This must be Megan and Drew's son."

Drew Dawson and his wife, Megan, lived on Dawson Ranch with Jenny, Adam and Abby.

Jenny shook her head and laughed. "Graham is fifteen months old now, and about twice the size of this little guy. Joshua is eight months old. He's Adam's and my son."

Autumn's heart twinged. She envied Jenny for the beautiful, happy family that she herself might never have.

Joshua smiled, his gray eyes bright, cheering Autumn right out of her blues. "He's adorable," she said.

"Uh-huh. We adopted him," Abby explained.

Jenny touched her daughter's shoulder lovingly. "That's right, sweetie." She turned to Autumn. "I hear you're working at Hope Ranch."

"This is my fourth day."

"Two of the boys living there, Justin and Noah, will be in my class this fall." Jenny shook her head. "Can you believe school starts in one month? This year I'll have four eighth-graders—more kids than in any other grade."

Autumn hadn't even thought about the two younger boys attending school in Saddlers Prairie, but of course, they would. Eric and Ty would no doubt ride the bus to the high school on the outskirts of town.

"Abby, honey, will you get me a package of noodles?"

her mother asked. "The wide ones we use." When the little girl skipped off, Jenny lowered her voice. "I hear the boys are a real handful."

Autumn thought about confiding in her about what had happened that morning, but wasn't sure she should. "I've known them just a few days, and they're testing me," she admitted. "They don't seem like bad kids, though."

"There you are," Cody said as he appeared with the cart.

His eyebrows tilted upward in question. No doubt he assumed she was still upset with him. But the cloud over his face lifted as he greeted Jenny.

"Autumn's been telling me a little bit about the boys," she explained as Autumn dropped her groceries in the cart.

"She's great with them." He leaned down to Joshua's level and shook the boy's chubby fingers. "Hey there, little man."

Joshua seemed delighted at the big male making a fuss over him. Autumn pictured Cody with his own infant. He'd make a great father.

"He's getting big," Cody said.

"Isn't he?" Jenny dabbed drool from her son's chin. "He has four teeth now."

Joshua started to fuss, and Jenny gave an apologetic smile. "He's about ready for his morning nap. I'd better go find Abby."

"Tell Adam hello," Cody said.

"I will. See you both later."

Jenny wheeled her cart away, leaving Autumn alone with Cody.

Rocking back on his heels, he eyed her warily. He'd

given up some of his valuable time to bring her here. Now he was tense and it was her fault.

This wasn't the ideal place for an apology, but it needed to be done.

AUTUMN'S SILENCE COULD only mean one thing—she was still upset with him. Wanting to make things right and coax back her smile, he cleared his throat. "Autumn, I—"

"Cody, I want—" she said at the same time.

"Mind if I go first?" Cody asked. She shook her head. There was no one else in the aisle, but to protect them against any unwanted eavesdroppers, he lowered his voice. "If I made a comment I shouldn't have earlier, I apologize."

"No, *I* owe *you* the apology." Avoiding eye contact, she rearranged some of the items in the cart. "I shouldn't have jumped down your throat like that. You're right, I am overly sensitive."

She straightened, her expressive eyes contrite.

Relieved, he blew out a breath. And wondered why a woman with her smarts thought she was less than bright. "I'll accept your apology if you accept mine."

"Okay."

Some twenty minutes later, when Autumn was satisfied that she had everything she needed, Cody pushed the brimming cart over to the checkout area.

"This is a great cookbook," Connie said, scanning the price. "I have the same one at home and I use it all the time."

Autumn mentioned several recipes she planned to try, and Connie suggested others her family liked.

"In the future, Autumn will be shopping without me," Cody said. "Please add her to the ranch account."

Connie was loading the last items into a box when

Cody's cell phone buzzed. He slid it from his hip pocket and checked the screen.

"It's my foreman. Take care of this for me, okay?" He handed Autumn several large bills before picking up. "Yeah, Doug?"

He listened with growing alarm. When he hung up moments later, Connie and Autumn were eyeing him with concern.

"We have to scoot, Autumn," he said. "A fire broke out in one of the north pastures."

IMPATIENT TO RETURN to the ranch and join his men, Cody wheeled the cart toward his truck in record time.

Autumn helped him load groceries into the truck bed. "Is it the same pasture the boys are in?"

He shook his head. "The one next to it. Doug and a bunch of the crew are over there, though."

"They know how to put out the fire, don't they?"

"Those things can be tricky. I need to be there. You can drive another time."

Autumn had barely shut her door before he peeled out of the parking lot.

"Was it the lightning strike we saw on the way here that set it off?" she asked.

"A different one. We're lucky it didn't hit the pasture where we're baling hay, but with everything so damn dry, the fire could easily spread." At that foreboding thought, he rode the gas pedal hard. The tires squealed and the truck lurched into warp speed.

Rather than shriek or yell at him to slow down Autumn silently braced her hands on the dash.

"If the forest service loans you one of their water pumpers, everything should be okay, though, right?" she asked after a moment.

Cody wasn't so sure, which was why he needed to get there ASAP. "The pumper's on its way, but if a wind kicks up…" He shook his head grimly. "Say a prayer that it doesn't."

In the distance, a thick black plume hovered over the burning field. As the truck drew closer, the smell of smoke seeped into the cab despite the closed windows.

Autumn sniffed and grimaced. "No one should breathe that stuff. Please tell me the boys have gone back to the house and are staying inside."

"Even if Doug tried to send them home, they wouldn't go. They'll be sticking around to help dig trenches to contain the fire. With the ground as hard and dry as it is, we need all the hands we can get. But don't worry, they'll wear wet bandannas over their noses and mouths, like everyone else."

"Noah and Justin are only fourteen. I don't like this at all," she said, sounding like an anxious mother.

Her reaction was sweet, but it didn't change anything. "Don't worry about them," he told her. "They're tougher than they look. And with the adrenaline racing through their veins, they'll have more than enough strength to pull their weight. I know I did when I used to help Phil during emergencies."

Autumn opened her mouth, and Cody braced for an argument he neither wanted nor had time for.

"How can I help?" she said instead.

He shouldn't have been surprised. Since she'd shown up at the ranch, she continually said or did the unexpected. "The boys and I will need food to keep us going," he said.

"And the crew?"

"They're responsible for themselves, and always have been. They probably brought their lunches along. The boys and I had planned to break for lunch at the house, but we won't be able to leave the blaze. You'll have to bring the food to us. You'll find ice packs in the big freezer in the basement. The coolers are down there, too."

"You want me to drive." Autumn caught her lower lip between her teeth.

"That's right. Take this truck or one of the Jeeps."

As soon as he braked to a stop in front of the house, he shut off the engine and tossed her the keys. "I'll grab a canteen and my bandanna, then take off. Can you handle the groceries by yourself?"

Before she'd even half unloaded the truck, Cody had saddled and mounted his horse, Diablo, and galloped off, leaving a cloud of dust in his wake.

PREOCCUPIED AND ANXIOUS, Autumn put away the groceries on automatic pilot. Fighting a fire was dangerous work—no task for teenage boys. The adrenaline rush Cody had mentioned lasted only so long, and she knew it.

As a teen, she'd once fought off a particularly aggressive boyfriend of Heather's. The fear that had sent Autumn racing across the prairie on a spring night long ago, and propelled her up a leafy cottonwood, had taken her only so far. By the time she felt safe again and shinnied down the trunk, she was shivering in the cool night air, and so drained of energy that trudging back home had taken monumental effort.

What would the boys do when their adrenaline highs wore off? Regardless what Cody had said, Autumn decided to offer them a ride back to the house.

Corralling the fire could take a while. Even if the crew had brought their lunches with them, they would need more to eat. She'd make enough sandwiches for everyone, something that wouldn't spoil in the heat.

After changing into sneakers and turning on the radio, she set to work. Time passed in a blur, marked only by news bulletins reporting a rash of lightning fires in the area. Autumn slathered peanut butter and jelly on bread until her fingers cramped and her back ached from hunching over. How did other housekeepers do it?

When she'd finally bagged the last sandwich, she wiped her forehead with the back of her hand and glanced longingly at a chair. But it was already past noon, and Cody and the boys were sure to be starving. They were probably wondering if she'd ever get her act together and show up with food.

She glanced at the sandwiches piled on every available surface. Six loaves of bread, most of a jumbo jar of peanut butter and an entire jar of jam—it looked like enough food for an army. Wouldn't they be surprised when she showed up with all this?

She had a lot to pack, and the truck would hold more than a Jeep. Sweating from the heat, she loaded the food and several coolers packed with bottled water into the truck bed.

After climbing into the driver's seat and adjusting the seat to fit her legs, Autumn turned the key. The engine purred to life. She put it in Drive and placed a tentative foot on the accelerator and the truck rolled forward. Here there were no speed limits, and no sheriff hiding in the bushes with his radar gun. But having never driven a truck before, she wasn't about to speed. She pulled carefully onto a crude dirt road forged from multiple tire tracks.

The smoke didn't seem as thick as before, but now blanketed a wide swath of air in its bad-smelling haze. Autumn drove across the uneven ground, wincing with every bounce. She braked to a stop a good fifty feet from the fire.

The ravenous flames had consumed a large area of grass and continued to sizzle and burn. In a rough circle around the fire, the boys and a half dozen ranch hands wielding shovels toiled away at the trenches they were digging. Dusty cowboy hats shielded their faces from the blistering sun, and damp-looking bandannas protected their noses and mouths from the smoke.

Nearby, Cody and two other hands directed thick hoses attached to a large container, sending hard sheets of water at the flames. Other men thwacked at smoking brush.

As soon as the boys spotted Autumn, they left their shovels sticking in the ground, tugged off their hats and bandannas and stumbled exhaustedly toward her. Their hair stuck up from their heads, and their sweaty faces were so coated in grime she hardly recognized them.

Yet despite the dirt and hours of backbreaking work better suited to men, they seemed somehow younger than they had this morning. Autumn puzzled over that before realizing why. Their facial expressions were different. Ty's tight-lipped resentment, Eric's spoiling-for-a-fight gangsta hostility, Noah's defiance and Justin's wariness—all had vanished.

Marveling at this change, she offered a warm smile before speaking loudly enough that she was heard by all. "I brought sandwiches and drinks for everyone."

She didn't miss the surprised murmurs, Cody's included.

"We'll eat in shifts," he said. "Justin, Noah, Ty and Eric, you're first. When you finish, four more."

The crew nodded and called out to each other, their camaraderie evident. They seemed to genuinely like and respect one another and especially Cody. Filled with admiration for him, Autumn opened the tailgate and gestured for the boys to help themselves.

They filled their arms with food and drink and sank down in the shade of the truck where they sat on the hard ground. After hours of shoveling, their hands were blistered.

Ty, Eric and Noah winced as they opened their sandwich bags. Justin remained stoic, but his hands had to hurt, too. Yet not one of them issued a single complaint. Thirsty and famished, they downed large bottles of water and demolished a good number of sandwiches, as well as enough chips and packaged cookies to feed ten boys.

"How are you guys holding up?" she asked when they began to slow down.

"Better now that I ate," Ty said.

Eric nodded and Justin shrugged.

Noah patted his belly. "Thanks."

None of them seemed to mind her company, which was a relief. Apparently, they'd forgiven her for this morning.

"If anyone is ready to quit and wants a ride back to the house, let me know," she offered.

As soon as the words left her lips, she knew she'd made a mistake.

Ty's open expression grew shuttered. He stood. "Now you think I'm a wimp *and* a thief," he accused in a voice everyone could hear.

"That's not it at all," Autumn said. "It's really hot out here and you've been hard at work for hours. *I'd* be ready to go home."

"We still need the boys' help," Cody called out.

"Comin' right now." Muttering and shaking his head, Eric pushed himself to his feet.

"We rode here on horses," Noah added. "We can't just leave them."

She hadn't thought about the animals.

Ty and Eric strode toward the trenches as if they couldn't wait to get away from her.

From the dirty looks Noah and Justin gave her before they followed the older boys, you'd have thought she'd accused them of committing a serious crime. Given her reaction to them this morning, in a way, she had.

Autumn sighed inwardly. Making things right with the boys wasn't going to be easy.

Chapter Eight

How did the men stand the heat and the stench of the smoke? Autumn quickly tired of both. By the time everyone but Cody and Doug had eaten, she was more than ready to return to the ranch, shower and drink a gallon of iced tea. She considered leaving the last of the food and water behind, but wanted a word with Cody first.

He handed the hose to a rangy cowboy named Jed. "The pumper's just about empty. Take the boys to the river with you and refill it."

"You got it, boss." Jed tipped his hat at Autumn. "Appreciate the lunch. Ty, Justin, Eric and Noah, help me load this thing into the truck."

After Jed and the boys had hefted the pumper into a beat-up truck and trundled off, Cody whipped off his baseball cap and thwacked it on his muscled thigh, sending dust flying. He and Doug ambled toward Autumn.

She hadn't met Doug yet. Soot darkened his face, but she guessed him to be in his late thirties. Wirier than Cody and not quite as tall, he was attractive all the same. But his grin didn't cause her heart to thud the way Cody's did.

Cody moved toward her. A light breeze had temporarily scattered the haze. With the endless, deep blue sky at his back, his dark, sweat-dampened hair seemed to shine and his shoulders appeared somehow broader. Autumn wasn't going to let herself feel anything for him, but there was no harm in appreciating the man. She smiled in greeting.

Unsmiling, without even a hint of curve to his lips, he nodded. Thanks to his mirrored sunglasses, she couldn't see his eyes, but she assumed he was unhappy that she'd offered the boys a ride back.

Autumn stiffened. "Go ahead, say what you need to say."

Doug veered away to talk with one of the other crew members, leaving Cody to approach her alone. He raised his eyebrows, looking more surprised than annoyed. "I'm too tired and hungry to talk. Will this do?"

He flashed a grin, his teeth looking extra white against his dirty skin.

Dear God, what a beautiful man.

Feelings washed over her, a sweet warmth born of strong physical attraction. If only she could see his eyes and discover if he felt it, too. She wanted to rip off his sunglasses, but it was probably best not to know.

Confused and flustered, heart fluttering, she blurted out her worries. "When I offered the boys a ride, I meant to help. Instead, I think I insulted them. I should have listened to you."

"You should have, but they'll get over it. You have to trust me, Autumn. If I think they've had enough, I'll send them home. They're doing okay, but they needed a break. That's why I sent them to the river with Jed."

He flipped the sunglasses up, propping them on his head. "Now can I eat?"

In the sunlight, the whiskey-brown of his eyes brightened to molten gold. Or maybe they shone because of her.

Autumn's wayward nerves began a sensual hum. Flustered, she brushed dirt from her skirt. "Help yourself."

As soon as she lowered her eyes from his, Cody slipped his sunglasses back into place, as if he was just as uncomfortable.

He beckoned to Doug. "Meet Autumn, our housekeeper. This is my foreman, Doug."

They exchanged greetings. Cody and Doug helped themselves to what was left of the food and water and sat in the shade of the truck.

Cody angled his head to look up at her. "Bringing enough food for everyone was a great idea."

Doug smiled. "I ate my own lunch long ago, and I sure appreciate these sandwiches."

Other men called out their thanks, making Autumn feel valued and important. A hole inside her filled, a place she hadn't even realized was empty.

"You're all working so hard out here," she said, waving her hand. "This was the least I could do."

Suddenly, her stomach growled, so loudly she was sure the cattle a few pastures away heard it.

Cody's eyebrows shot up comically. "Have *you* eaten?"

Not since the toast and a few sneaked spoonfuls of peanut butter.

"There's still plenty left." He patted the ground beside him. "Join us."

Given her unwanted feelings for Cody, Autumn preferred to keep a distance. She hesitated.

"Afraid of getting dirty?" he asked around a mouthful of sandwich.

"It's not that. A short skirt makes sitting on the ground a little awkward." Her cheeks burned.

"Doesn't bother me," one of the hands called out, chuckling.

Cody gave him a dirty look and handed Autumn his bandanna. "Put this over your lap."

She sat down, covering her exposed knees and thighs with the cloth.

After wolfing down a sandwich, Cody pulled off his sunglasses and wiped his face with the hem of his shirt. She caught a glimpse of his lean belly. When she glanced up, his gaze was locked on her.

She quickly glanced away. "I heard on the radio that there are lightning fires all over the area."

"I was afraid of that." Cody shook his head. "We're making decent progress here. I just hope other ranchers are doing as well."

"With our bellies full, we'll be even more effective," Doug said. "We should have this thing put out in no time."

Cody drained a bottle of water and then brushed his palms together. "Let's get back to it."

He offered Autumn a hand up, his callused grip firm and warm. "Thanks again for what you did today, Autumn. You're the best."

She knew that last part was just a figure of speech, yet her heart all but melted. Was she that hard up?

"Should I bring more food later?" she asked.

Cody shook his head. "You've done enough for one day. Doug's right—if the wind holds off and we continue to make good progress, we should be home in a few hours."

When they'd no doubt all be hungry again. Overwhelmed at the thought, Autumn gave a weary nod.

"Why don't you pick up a couple dozen extra-large pizzas for dinner tonight," Cody said. "The number of the pizza place is hanging on the side of the fridge. They have my credit card information on file."

"A couple dozen?" she repeated, to make sure she hadn't misheard. No one could be that hungry.

"Enough for the whole crew. There's a pen and pad of paper in the glove compartment of the truck for you to write down the orders."

While Cody and Doug packed the lunch trash into the truck bed, Autumn jotted down the pizza toppings the men wanted. Cody told her what he and the boys liked.

"It's a huge order, so you should phone it in right away," he said. "As soon as we head back to the house, I'll call you."

CODY HAD MISCALCULATED how long it would take them to extinguish the fire. By the time the stubborn thing finally gave up and died, the sun was slanting toward the horizon and he was bushed. Before mounting Diablo, he phoned Autumn.

She answered on the first ring. "Cody?"

"Yep. We're heading back."

"Thank God," she said, sounding relieved. "I was getting worried."

He liked that she cared, and couldn't help smiling. "See you soon."

Long before he was close enough to make out her face, he saw her waiting out front, ponytail blowing in the breeze. Nearby, the tailgate of the truck stood open, revealing neat stacks of white pizza boxes.

One glance at those long legs, bare shoulders and full breasts, and his tired body stirred to life. Which wasn't surprising. Whenever a ranch emergency ended, Cody rode home hungry for a woman's love.

She lifted a hand and waved.

Some of the crew whipped off their hats and waved back, and more than one pleased murmur passed among them. The boys, too, seemed glad to see her—and those pizzas.

"She's a honey," Pete, one of the ranch hands, said. "If I weren't dating Celine, I'd ask her out."

Cody frowned. He wasn't interested in Autumn, but he didn't want any of his guys getting ideas about asking her out, either.

As the rest of the group spurred their horses forward, Cody hung back with Doug.

"That Autumn's something special," the foreman commented, in a voice too low for anyone but Cody to hear.

He was beginning to agree. He still couldn't get over her thoughtfulness earlier. Bringing extra sandwiches for Doug and the rest of the crew had earned her untold gratitude.

"Ty says she can't cook," Doug went on. "My Joan cooks like a dream. When I called her a little while ago, I told her about Autumn. Joan offered to give her some cooking lessons."

Autumn might appreciate that. "That'd be nice," Cody said. He clucked and kneed Diablo into a gallop.

Dismounting near the truck, he thanked the men for their efforts. He left Autumn to hand out the pizzas, while he and the boys led the horses into the barn. When the animals had been stabled, brushed, fed and watered, Cody gathered the boys around.

"I'm proud of all of you for the hard work you did today," he said. "Men's work."

Their chests seemed to swell with pride. They also looked utterly beat.

"Now, go take a shower, and I'll see you in the kitchen afterward for pizza."

A little while later, with all the grime and soot washed off his body, Cody dug into his pizza. Seated across the table, between Noah and Ty, Autumn toyed with the garden salad she'd made. She hadn't wanted to join them, but Cody had insisted. She wasn't eating much of her pizza, either. Her cheeks and shoulders were on the pink side and he wondered if she'd gotten too much sun today. He was about to ask if she felt sick when she cleared her throat.

"Boys—I want to apologize. Offering you a ride back to the house when you were in the middle of fighting the fire was an insult to you all. You're a lot more grown-up and responsible than I realized."

She blew out a breath. Nobody's expression changed, and no one said anything. In fact, the room went dead silent.

"I'm also sorry for my behavior this morning," she went on, her gaze including each boy. "When I was growing up, I kept my babysitting money in a jar in my room. My mom used to 'borrow' from it without asking, and I guess I'm still a little skittish. But that's no excuse for my knee-jerk reaction." She bit her lip. "I know that none of you would steal from me."

Her apology was so heartfelt that Cody's chest hurt. He gave her a barely perceptible nod of approval, and some of the anxiety pinching her features faded.

Noah bit into his pizza, which he'd seemed to have temporarily forgotten. A moment later, he gave her a puzzled look. "Why didn't you open a savings account and put your money there instead? That's what Cody makes us do with half of everything we earn."

Cody nodded. "The bulk of my money is in the bank."

"That's a good idea, and you're lucky Cody's teaching you to save," Autumn said. "I didn't even know I could open an account until I was on my own."

She attempted a smile that no one returned. The boys

all understood, all had parents who'd never taught them about banks or any number of things most families took for granted.

"I used to have an account, but I closed it when I left town," she added. "Eventually, I'll open another, but for now, all my money is in that can." She placed a finger over her lips. "Please don't tell anyone."

"I won't," Noah said.

Ty shook his head. "The rest of us won't, either."

Autumn wiped her brow. "Now I can eat. If you're not too tired or hungry to talk, I'd love to hear more about how you finally stopped the fire."

The mood in the room lightened considerably as the boys proudly shared their accomplishments.

"Digging that trench with the other guys was cool," Justin volunteered. "But my arms, back and legs sure are sore." He glanced at his palms. "My hands hurt, too."

"I noticed those blisters at lunch," Autumn said. "When I picked up the pizzas, I bought a salve that should help. I didn't know if you had any in the house, Cody."

He wasn't sure, either, as he rarely used the stuff. Her thoughtfulness continued to amaze him. "I appreciate that," he said. He glanced at each boy. "Today I caught glimpses of the fine men you'll be someday. What I said in the barn bears repeating—I'm proud of you all."

"Me, too," Autumn seconded.

Unused to praise, the boys shifted in their seats.

"Tell me, do men eat ice-cream sandwiches?" she asked.

A unanimous "yes!" filled the room.

Twenty minutes later, three empty ice-cream-sandwich cartons filled the recycling bin.

"Did everyone get enough to eat?" Autumn asked.

Ty sat back in his chair and patted his belly. "You're okay, Autumn."

"The pizza and ice-cream sandwiches were top gun," Eric said.

Noah nodded. "So was lunch."

"You put a lot of PB & J in the sandwiches, just how I like them," Justin said, eyes on his empty plate.

Autumn's whole face seemed to glow with pleasure, dazzling Cody. Once again she'd worked her magic on the boys and on him.

"I'm just glad you're all home and in one piece," she told everyone, but her eyes were on him.

For one long moment their gazes held. The boys probably noticed, but Cody couldn't look away. The urge to kiss her was so strong, he gripped the seat of his chair to keep from standing, rounding the table and reaching for her. Thank God for the boys. If not for them, he'd surely do something he'd regret.

Flushing, Autumn smoothed her ice-cream wrapper self-consciously.

Cody stacked his dishes and stood. "Time to clean up."

Without a single grumble, the boys scraped back their chairs.

"You all worked so hard today," Autumn said. "I'll take care of this mess. Go into the great room, put up your feet and relax. As soon as I finish the dishes, I'll bring you some popcorn."

Ty shook his head. "I'm going to bed."

The other boys gave weary nods.

"No TV tonight?" Autumn asked, looking incredulous.

Cody shook his head. "They're beat, and so am I. By the way, I want you boys to take tomorrow off and relax."

"You mean we get to sleep in?" Eric grinned. "I can handle that."

"I'll see you all in the morning," Autumn said as they plodded wearily toward the hallway. "Now that I have a new alarm clock, I promise not to oversleep."

Noah laughed. "But we will."

Like the boys, Cody intended to turn in soon, but not just yet. "You passed a huge test today," he said when they were out of earshot.

Autumn looked confused. "I thought I failed one."

"This morning, you did. This afternoon you redeemed yourself and then some. Thanks again for lunch."

"You're welcome. By the way, I used up most of the bread. I'll have to go back to Spenser's tomorrow and pick up more."

"You're okay with driving yourself now?"

"I think so."

"That was easy. We keep the keys to all the vehicles on the side cabinet in the barn. Anytime you need to go someplace, just take whatever's available. That includes weekends."

"You'd let me take a car over the weekend?"

"How else will you get away from here? Just let me know first."

"Thanks, Cody."

They smiled at each other, and the urge to kiss her grabbed him again. Hard.

His grin slipped. Autumn's eyes darkened with desire before she turned away. His body tense, he stood and began to stack the dinner plates.

"Leave it, Cody. There isn't that much to do, and I really don't mind."

He needed to get away from her, and ought to let her clean up alone. Yet he stayed right where he was. "If we do it together, we'll finish in under five minutes. You rinse and I'll load the dishwasher."

He was disposing of the pizza boxes when he remembered what his foreman had mentioned earlier. "Doug said that his wife might be able to give you some cooking lessons."

"You told him I can't cook?"

"Ty did. You'll like Joan. She's nice."

They worked in comfortable silence. Every so often, Cody caught a whiff of Autumn's lilac perfume.

Beat clear to his bones, he was ready to head upstairs. He dried his hands and opened his mouth to tell her goodnight. "It's early yet, and you mentioned popcorn," he said instead. "Interested in watching a DVD?"

She looked surprised. "Sure, but don't you need to go to bed?"

Oh, he wanted to be in bed, all right—with Autumn beside him. Make that under him.

If he was smart, he'd walk out of the kitchen now and head upstairs. Instead he reached for a big bowl in the cabinet. "I'll make the popcorn and you pick the movie."

Chapter Nine

"Are you sure you want to watch this?" Cody asked, eyeing the thriller Autumn had selected. He placed the popcorn and two cold beers on the coffee table. "I figured you for the romantic-comedy type."

She was, but a love story seemed like something a couple might watch, and she and Cody were hardly that. "I enjoy them, but this has been a really long day and we're both tired. We need something to keep us on our toes. Otherwise, I just might fall asleep on the sofa and miss the whole thing."

That wasn't quite true. She was strangely keyed up. She'd never imagined the two of them alone, watching a movie together.

Not that it meant anything.

Or maybe it did.

In the kitchen she'd caught Cody looking at her as if he wanted to kiss her. She foolishly wanted him to—just as she had a few nights ago. No, tonight she wanted his kiss even more.

Common sense warned her not to let that happen.

He loaded the DVD player. "If this movie lives up to its reputation, neither of us will be blinking, never mind falling asleep."

The sectional sofa was easily big enough for five

adults. Autumn plunked herself down at one end, giving him plenty of space to spread out a nice, safe distance from her.

But he sat down smack in the middle, positioned the bowl beside him and patted the cushion. "You can't reach the popcorn all the way over there."

When Autumn waffled, he gave her a teasing grin. "I promise not to bite."

Against her better judgment, she changed seats. The movie previews began. She usually enjoyed watching those, but tonight she couldn't focus, couldn't have later described a preview to save her life. She was too aware that Cody was less than an arm's length away, close enough for her to reach out and run her fingers through his hair....

Well, she never had showed much common sense.

Determined to keep her mind off the man beside her and pay attention to the movie—or at least pretend to—Autumn munched on popcorn, sipped her beer and kept her gaze glued to the screen. The movie started off with a bang, and in no time, she was sucked into the story.

Cody seemed equally drawn into the unfolding events. In the middle of a particularly scary scene, he paused the action. "Sure you want to watch this? I don't want you having nightmares."

"I'm okay," she said. "Why, are you scared?"

"Nah." A moment later, he gave her a sheepish look. "A little." He pushed Play and the movie continued.

That big, masculine Cody Naylor admitted to being scared only made her like him all the more. Stifling a smile, she reached for the popcorn—at the same instant as Cody. Their hands collided and buttery kernels spilled onto the cushion.

"Oops." Chuckling, he paused the movie again. He

scooped popcorn from the sofa cushions and popped it into his mouth.

Instead of restarting the DVD, he stood. "By now it'll be cooler outside, and I like the night breeze. Mind if I turn off the air and open the slider?"

"Not at all."

Seconds later, the pleasant sound of crickets filled the room.

"Come see the moon," Cody said.

If that didn't sound like an invitation to a kiss, Autumn didn't know what did. She hesitated, but her legs pushed her up and propelled her forward. He opened the screen and they stepped into the night, out of the light coming from the interior of the house.

The soft evening breeze smelled fresh and free of smoke. Overhead, the moon hung in the darkening sky like a giant golden ball.

Autumn stared in wonder. "How beautiful."

"Yeah," Cody said, looking at her instead of the moon, his heavy-lidded gaze making her shiver. After a moment, he returned his attention to the sky. "It's almost full tonight."

He stood far enough away that they weren't quite touching, yet close enough that she felt the heat from his body and smelled the clean scent of his shower soap.

The electricity between them was almost palpable, and every cell in her body arched toward him in silent anticipation of his touch.

But nothing happened.

Which was for the best, she told herself though her entire body screamed for her to kiss him. She had to get away from him before she did something she would regret.

Stepping back, she opened the sliding door with trembling hands. "I think I should go to bed now."

She all but ran toward the kitchen, with Cody silently following her. As soon as he entered the room, he shut the door behind him.

"Autumn."

He packed so much emotion into her name—a heartfelt plea that expressed all the desire and confusion she felt.

He reached for her and she walked into his arms.

CODY'S NEED TO taste Autumn bordered on a desperation he didn't understand and couldn't fight. He cupped her face between his hands, kissed her closed eyelids and brushed his lips over hers. A shudder shook her, and for a long moment he feared he'd made a mistake. Mustering all the strength he had, he kept the kiss gentle and tentative until she twined her arms around his neck and kissed him back.

Her lips were warm, eager. A thrill jolted through him. Angling his head, he deepened the kiss, sliding his tongue into her welcoming mouth. She tasted of popcorn and beer and a sweetness that was hers alone.

Her soft breasts pressed against his chest. His hungry body hardened painfully and demanded more. Molding his palms to her hips, he anchored her against his erection.

He wanted to strip off her panties, pull up her little skirt and bury himself in her warmth, right there on the kitchen floor. He slid one hand up the back of her incredibly smooth thigh.

Bad move. She stiffened.

"Don't, Cody." She batted his hand away and pulled out of his arms.

With effort, he shook the fog from his brain. What was he doing, fooling around with Autumn? She was his housekeeper, for God's sake.

Getting involved with her was risky and could jeopardize what he wanted and the boys needed—for her to stay the full sixty days.

He should apologize, only he wasn't sorry. Which just went to show how crazy in lust he was. "I have no idea why I did that," he said.

"I know, and it's okay—I wanted you to."

Not exactly words to cool down by.

Looking stunned, Autumn smoothed her top over her voluptuous hips. Womanly softness that had fitted perfectly against him... Cody swallowed and shifted his weight.

"At least we got it out of our systems."

Maybe *she* had. Cody only wanted more. He cleared his throat. "Tomorrow's another long day, and we both need our rest."

Autumn nodded. Her lips were slightly red from his kisses, and strands of hair had worked loose from her ponytail. Without thinking, he tucked them behind her ears. "Unless you want to try that again."

She glanced toward the alcove that led to her apartment. Keeping his hands at his sides, he waited for her to walk away from him. But she surprised him and stepped back into his arms.

"Just one more," she whispered, her eyes impossibly luminous. "But kissing only." Her eyelids fluttered shut.

Cody noticed a tiny mole right below where her lashes flirted with her cheek. He wanted to kiss it, but he was more interested in tasting that mouth again.

What was supposed to be one kiss melted into another

and another, until desire sizzled in his blood. Somehow, he found the strength to let her go and back away.

"Good night, Autumn."

She gave a dazed nod.

Hot and hungry, and shaking his head over his behavior, Cody left the kitchen. He hadn't intended to kiss her again, but the simple act of tucking her silky hair behind the delicate shells of her ears and watching desire bloom in her eyes had sapped his willpower.

In the great room, he put the DVD away with unsteady hands. The strength and force of his hunger for Autumn astonished him. He hadn't been this aroused in longer than he could remember. Maybe never.

He couldn't trust himself around her and knew he was playing with fire. From now on, he would avoid being alone with her. If they somehow ended up that way, he would keep his distance. He sure as hell wouldn't touch her.

As addictive as kissing Autumn was, any repeats were out of the question. Period.

Cody shut off the lights and climbed the stairs to his bedroom.

INSIDE HER APARTMENT, still warm and tingly inside, Autumn sagged against the door. Eyes closed, she remembered the checked strength of Cody's arms cradling her against his solid body. His big, hot hands grasping her hips, pulling her hard against his erection. He hadn't so much as grazed her breasts, yet her nipples felt swollen and sensitive.

The sensual feel of his rough fingers skimming up the back of her thigh… Heat and longing had dampened her panties, made her ache for so much more.

Fresh hunger surged through her, and a moan slipped

from her lips, a sound of desire and need she had no business making.

She wanted Cody more than she'd ever desired anyone—and she'd been here less than a week. What was the matter with her? She didn't want to feel this way. She was supposed to be taking a break from men.

She was a fool, making a stupid mistake. Snapping back to reality, she pushed herself away from the door. From this moment on, no matter how badly she wanted to kiss Cody—and more—she wasn't going to act on her feelings.

By the time she went into the bathroom to get ready for bed, her common sense had kicked back in. The men who were usually attracted to her weren't exactly guys with sterling qualities.

That good, decent Cody Naylor desired her was a new and heady experience. But Autumn knew she wasn't smart enough or pretty enough to hold him for long. She barely had her high school diploma—she could never be enough.

As interested as he was now, sooner or later he was bound to grow tired of her. What if he decided he didn't want her around anymore? She could wind up in jail.

Autumn stared at herself in the bathroom mirror. If she wanted to avoid that and prove how different she was from Heather, she needed to keep this job the full sixty days.

Which meant that from now on, kissing Cody, and anything else that wasn't part of her job description, was out.

Yet even as she reasoned with herself, part of her already looked forward to kissing him again.

Pressing her lips tightly together, she firmly pushed

her feelings so deep inside, they wouldn't dare bubble back to the surface.

Cody Naylor was off-limits. She would *not* kiss him again.

Chapter Ten

Cody woke up before dawn Friday, his thoughts on Autumn and how good she'd felt in his arms. Her unfettered participation, the sweet torture of her body molded to his in all the right places…

Heat stirred in him yet again. He snickered at his hard-on. Apparently it hadn't gotten the message that he was staying away from her.

A short while later, shaved, showered, dressed and ready to start the day, he pulled on a pair of socks and padded downstairs. With the boys sleeping in, the house was eerily quiet.

After months of living with them, he'd grown used to their company and the bustle that surrounded them. Not for the first time, he wondered how Phil had been able to stand the silence with his wife dead and the foster kids grown and gone. He'd always claimed that Cody's showing up at the ranch had been a godsend. Cody finally understood.

The kitchen was dark and quiet, and he assumed that Autumn, too, was asleep. Good thing. Given this crazy hunger of his, he was better off not seeing her just now.

Working quietly, he started the coffeemaker. He pulled a frying pan from the drawer under the oven, causing the rest of the pots and pans in there to clang and bang something awful. Fearing he'd awakened Autumn, he froze and cocked an ear toward her door.

To his relief, he didn't hear a sound.

What did she wear to bed? he wondered, pulling breakfast items from the fridge. He pictured her in an oversize T-shirt. Imagined slipping into her double bed and waking her with a kiss. Her eyes, still foggy with sleep, would slowly focus and darken with hunger. Then he'd *really* wake her up.

Tense and hard all over again, he was thankful she wasn't around. And decided he'd make a breakfast sandwich to bring with him, as well as pack himself a lunch. He wouldn't come back until dinner.

A long day of haying should clear his head and calm his body. Thank God it was Friday. She was off all weekend. With any luck, he wouldn't see much of her until Monday.

AUTUMN'S NEW ALARM clock blasted her from a deep sleep. Bleary-eyed, she shut it off. She'd slept like the dead, dreamless and unmoving. Through a crack in the drapes, she saw that the sky was the vivid pink of sunrise.

Stretching and yawning, she sat up. As her fogginess faded, images and thoughts flooded her mind. Last night she'd kissed Cody—twice.

With a groan, she reached for the spare pillow and hugged it close. A pathetic substitute for the warm man she wanted, but a whole lot safer.

The inviting aroma of freshly brewed coffee seeped under the door, filling the apartment. Cody must be awake. And here she'd thought she'd be up first this morning. Not quite ready to face him, Autumn stepped into the shower. She took her time getting dressed and fixing her hair.

She was thinking about staying in her apartment
a while longer when she caught herself and frowned.
Hiding from him was ridiculous. Besides, he needed his
lunch.

It was probably better to face him now, without an au-
dience. She would explain that last night was a mistake
that couldn't happen again, and they'd move on.

Her stomach churning, she opened her door and
passed through the alcove.

To her surprise, Cody wasn't in the kitchen. She spotted a hastily scribbled note propped against the toaster.
"Gone until dinner. Remind the boys to water and weed
the vegetable garden. Otherwise, they're free for the day."

She wouldn't have to face him until six. Relief loosened her tense shoulders and calmed her stomach. A full
day away from him was just what she needed.

Unfortunately, she hadn't had a chance to pack his
lunch. From now on, she would make all lunches after
dinner, and store them in the refrigerator.

After dinner tonight, before her weekend off officially
began, she would talk with Cody about the mistake they'd
made, and clear up any misunderstandings. Hopefully,
that would take care of the problem.

AUTUMN HAD JUST returned from Spenser's with several
loaves of bread and a fresh jar of jam when Noah and
Justin tramped into the kitchen, lugging their garden basket between them. Ty and Eric had already weeded and
watered, leaving the younger boys to pick.

So much produce, and there was still plenty left over
from the past few days. "What am I supposed to do with
all this?" she asked.

"Like we're supposed to know," Justin mumbled, any
warmth from yesterday having vanished.

Would he ever grow comfortable with her?

"You could give some to the crew," Noah suggested.

"That's not a bad idea," Autumn said, impressed. "I'm going to clean the kitchen and great room today, but you lucky guys are free for the rest of the day. What are your plans?"

"We're all gonna ride our horses down to the river and swim," Noah replied.

"Have you cleared that with Cody?" Autumn asked.

The boy nodded. "We go there all the time."

"What time do you want lunch?"

"Don't worry, we'll stay out of your way. We'll take it with us."

"I don't mind at all if you're here, Noah," Autumn said. The boy looked skeptical. "I mean it. I'll clean around you."

"We'd rather eat at the river."

"A picnic it is. I'll pack something for you."

"Could you do it now? We want to go soon."

Ten minutes later, all four boys entered the kitchen with their backpacks, where they stowed the drinks and sack lunches Autumn had hastily put together.

"When will you be back?" she asked.

"When we get through," Ty said, as surly as ever.

And not so much as a thank-you for his lunch. Like Justin, he seemed to have forgotten about the bonding that had taken place last night. Autumn bit back a disheartened sigh. "Don't stay out too long, and wear your hats and sunscreen."

"No effin' duh." Eric made a sarcastic sound. "We ain't stupid."

The telling comment confirmed that others no doubt considered Eric to be just that. Having been there herself multiple times, Autumn quickly reassured him. "It's just a reminder, Eric. I don't think you're stupid."

"Yeah, right," Ty scoffed. "Like you'd even know."

Was this yet another test? "I know because you chose to come to the ranch rather than live on the streets," she said.

While the boys digested that, she changed the subject. "Here's a heads-up for you—I've decided to clean your bedrooms and bathroom on Mondays."

Ty's eyes narrowed. "You don't trust us to go into your apartment. Why should we trust you in our rooms?"

Hadn't she already apologized? Autumn wanted to scream in frustration, but Cody had warned her that she'd be tested many times.

"Because my mom was always looking through my private stuff, and I hated it," she explained. "I would never snoop through someone else's things. I'll respect your privacy, and that's a promise." She made eye contact with each of the boys. "How about this—if you don't want me to see something of yours, put it in a dresser drawer or in a box in your closet."

Despite her earnestness, not one of them seemed convinced. Mentally, she threw up her hands. "Cleaning is part my job, but hey, if you'd rather do it instead, then *I'll* go swimming on Monday."

Ty quickly backtracked. "Uh, that's okay. You go ahead."

"I *want* you to clean our room, Autumn." Noah glanced at Justin. "Don't you?"

"If she means the part about not snooping around."

"I do." Autumn made an *X* on her chest. "Cross my heart."

Eric, Noah and Justin looked to Ty, who eyed her warily. "We'll see. Let's get outta here."

"Have fun," Autumn said, forcing a bright tone.

You'd think they'd be happy about having most of the day off to play, but no. They trudged into the utility room, their footsteps as heavy as those of prisoners headed for the gallows.

But seconds before the side door closed behind them, she heard laughter and lighthearted chatter. Apparently the misery they projected was an act for her benefit.

Silence filled the house, interrupted only by the soft whir of the air conditioner. Despite the boys' surly moods, Autumn missed the noise. She changed into her cleaning uniform—cutoffs and an oversize T-shirt—and brought the portable radio into the kitchen. She turned the volume up high for company. A nasally male singer belted out a country-and-western song about lost love.

Eager to show Cody and the boys that even if she couldn't cook very well, she could clean with the best of them, Autumn compiled the needed supplies and set to work. She quickly realized the job was much bigger than she'd thought. Cody and the boys kept the kitchen and utility rooms reasonably tidy, but both needed a thorough scrubbing.

By the time she finished the two rooms, her stomach was empty and complaining. After breaking for lunch, she worked her way through the powder room, dining room and hallway that led to the great room. Like the kitchen, it needed a thorough going-over.

She was finishing up when the grandfather clock chimed four o'clock. Autumn glanced at it in surprise. More hours had passed than she'd anticipated, but everything except the boys' rooms was spick-and-span. A good feeling, indeed.

She hated to dirty up the sparkling kitchen, but it was time to change clothes and start dinner.

AROUND NOON, CODY, Doug and the four hands helping them with the haying stopped for lunch. Despite the Herculean task of cutting and baling the unruly hay grass before it dried out too much, they were making good progress.

Grouped under the shade of a broad cottonwood, they brought out their lunches. Zeke, Moses and the other hands had nonperishable sack lunches like Cody's, but Doug had brought a cooler complete with dry ice to keep his food cold. His sandwich, a thick roast beef concoction dressed with lettuce, cheese and tomato, made Cody's mouth water.

"That's a good-looking sandwich," he said.

"My better half made it from the other night's leftovers." Doug eyed Cody's PB & J. "I see Autumn gave you the same as yesterday."

"I made this one myself." Though if she'd packed his lunch, she'd likely have given him the same thing. "Trust me, this is a damn sight better than any of the dinner leftovers at my place."

"You need a competent cook, Cody," Zeke said. "Better yet, a wife."

The men dug into their lunches, leaving Cody with his thoughts. For a little while several years ago he'd thought he'd found the right woman for him. They were talking marriage and about to go ring shopping. Then one night he'd overheard Heidi tell her best friend that she didn't love him and was with him only for the perks. When he'd confronted her, she'd tearfully admitted the truth.

After Cody had sold his business and come back to look after Phil, his foster dad had pushed him to keep looking. "I know you don't trust easily, but it's been a couple of years since Heidi—time to get on with your life," he'd said. "You're thirty-four now, and you need a wife and kids so you don't end up a lonely old man like me."

Cody had been thinking about that ever since, and found the idea growing on him. He was ready to fall in love again. But in Saddlers Prairie there weren't a lot of available women to choose from, let alone one eager to move into a house with four foster teenage boys. He wasn't sure how to go about finding someone. Maybe he'd tried online dating, in the future. At this point, taking care of the boys and finding a permanent housekeeper were keeping him busy enough.

"Joan will be calling Autumn soon about that cooking lesson," Doug was saying. "Then you'll have your own roast beef leftovers for lunch."

Cody hoped so. Suddenly, his cell phone buzzed. Lifting his hip, he slid the thing from his pocket. Judge Niemeyer's name appeared on the screen.

The judge had been a longtime friend of Phil's and was a generous supporter of Hope Ranch. "I'd better take this," Cody said, pushing himself to his feet.

"Hey, Judge." Adjusting his baseball cap to shade his eyes, he moved out of earshot. "What's up?"

"Thought I'd check on things. Autumn's just about through her first week at the ranch. How's she working out?"

Images of her in his arms, sharing some of the hottest kisses of his life, filled Cody's head. His body started to stir. He frowned. "She's doing all right."

"Word's out that she can't cook."

Cody wasn't surprised that Judge had heard about that. In a town the size of Saddlers Prairie, news spread with amazing speed. "She wants to learn, though. My foreman's wife has offered to teach her."

"By all means, encourage that. How is she getting on with the boys?"

"Overall they seem to like her, but you know how that goes." Judge knew all about how the boys had tested the previous housekeepers, and the problems that had caused. He knew Cody hadn't been able to find a permanent housekeeper.

"Yesterday was interesting." Cody told him about the fire and described how Autumn had brought enough food for the whole crew. "She impressed everyone."

"That sounds promising," the older man said. "Do you think she'll stick around the full sixty days?"

Cody thought about that. Autumn had reassured him several times that she intended to stay. She'd weathered some rough patches and was still here, which he took as a positive sign. But the boys weren't through testing her, and she could still change her mind.

"Time will tell," he said.

"Keep me posted."

They both clicked off.

Cautiously optimistic and hoping like hell she wouldn't let them down, Cody rejoined his crew.

Chapter Eleven

Autumn studied the casserole instructions in her new cookbook. With its easy-to-follow steps, the recipe looked simple enough, but putting it all together still seemed daunting. She hated the thought of another dinner fiasco, and prayed she wouldn't disappoint Cody and the boys again—especially after her promise to improve.

She paused for a moment before getting started, and stole a glance out the window. The air seemed to shimmer with heat. Even with the AC keeping the house cool, it seemed awfully hot to turn on the oven. At least that was the excuse she used to change her mind about the casserole.

A large, covered barbecue that sat on the brick patio out back. Why not make life easy and grill hamburgers tonight?

Not that she had ever grilled anything. Back in high school, a few months before she'd moved out of her mother's house, Heather's then live-in boyfriend had fancied himself a master barbecuer. He'd shown Autumn how to fire up the grill and keep it clean. She'd watched him cook hamburger patties many times. Really, there was nothing to it.

In the pantry, she found charcoal and lighter fluid. She set them outside and uncovered the grill, which was clean and ready to use. After only spending a few minutes outside, she was already uncomfortably hot. She envied the boys their afternoon at the river.

She went back inside and was considering changing into cutoffs and a T-shirt when the landline rang.

Thinking it might be Cody, she tightened her ponytail and tugged down the hem of her blouse. As if he could see her through the phone.

"Hope Ranch, this is Autumn," she said, sounding breathless even to herself.

"Hi, Autumn. This is Joan Tyee, Doug's wife. Am I catching you at a bad time?"

Disappointment sluiced through her before she brushed it away. Cody was out haying. He wouldn't phone unless something was wrong.

"Now is a perfect time," she replied. "Cody mentioned that you'd be calling." Tucking the phone between her ear and her shoulder, she opened the refrigerator and pulled out a pitcher of iced tea. "I was just coming in from the patio. I've decided to grill burgers tonight."

"It'll be a good evening for that. I just thought I'd call and say hello and welcome to the ranch."

Autumn smiled into the phone. "Thank you."

"So, how do you like taking care of Cody and the boys?"

Autumn thought about the kisses she'd shared with Cody, and the boys with their hostile attitudes. The intimidating tasks of feeding five voracious males twice a day and keeping the big house clean.

"It's different," she summarized. "I've never had a job like this, and I'm learning as I go." She wasn't going to say another word, but when Joan made a sympathetic sound, Autumn added, "I've already made mistakes I wish I could go back and fix."

Kissing Cody, for one. As right as his arms had felt around her, kissing him was a one-way ticket to trouble. Unintentionally insulting the boys was equally bad. She bit her lip. "I don't want to mess up again."

Joan laughed. "Believe me, we've all made our share of mistakes. Nothing about ranching is easy, and you have those boys to deal with, too. Managing the house is a huge job in itself."

Autumn liked the woman's laugh, and found herself smiling again. "So I'm discovering."

"Doug says you wouldn't mind a cooking lesson."

"Mind? I need all the help I can get." Truth be told, Autumn wasn't sure she could even grill the hamburgers without ruining them.

"I thought we could get together tomorrow," Joan said. "Unless you have something planned?"

Autumn's weekend was as empty as the Montana sky on an August afternoon. Cody had offered her the use of one of his vehicles for personal use, but where would she go? Sherry had plans with her boyfriend, and most of Autumn's other friends had either moved out of town or were busy with their families. Even Heather was still away.

"Nothing planned but sleeping in," she said.

"Lucky you. I work part-time at the insurance office. I'm supposed to get weekends off, but a ranch foreman's wife rarely gets the chance to sit down and relax."

Wife. A title Autumn had always dreamed of, but given her track record so far, who knew if she'd ever find the right man? She might never get married.

"Doug is working tomorrow," Joan went on. "This time of year, he almost always does. Why don't you come over to our place for a cup of coffee and a cooking lesson?"

"I'd love to. What time?"

"My morning is packed with the usual household chores, so how about right after lunch?"

"I'll be there," Autumn said, looking forward to the visit. "What should I bring?"

"Tell me what you want to learn to cook, and we'll make a grocery list."

"Something hearty enough for a hungry man and four teenage boys who are always starving," Autumn said. "Cody and the boys like sweets, too, so maybe a dessert of some kind?"

"I know the perfect casserole-lasagna."

"You don't think the weather is too hot for lasagna?"

"As long as the air is on and the temperature in the kitchen is comfortable, they'll be happy. Do you have as much zucchini as we do?"

"Tons, plus more green beans, tomatoes and lettuce than we'll ever eat." Autumn mentioned Noah's idea about giving some of the produce to the rest of the crew.

"They share a yard and it isn't big enough for a garden, so they'll love that. If you're interested, I could teach you to can some of those vegetables for the winter," Joan said. "We'll save that for another lesson. This time we'll make lasagna, garlic bread, and for dessert, chocolate zucchini bars."

Autumn's mouth watered. "That sounds great. But will the food keep until Monday?"

"You bet. You can store everything in the fridge, but if I were you, I'd hide it all in the freezer so it doesn't get eaten over the weekend. If Cody and the boys are anything like Doug, by Tuesday, you'll be whipping up a second batch of the zucchini bars."

The very idea of something she baked disappearing so quickly pleased Autumn.

"Grab a pen and paper and we'll make a grocery list."

Joan dictated the list of ingredients and provided Autumn with directions to her house. Most of the crew lived in trailers on the far side of the ranch, but Joan and Doug had a cottage with a yard, one of the perks that came with the foreman's job.

By the time the call ended, Autumn felt happier than she had in ages. Who needed to worry over a recipe when she could learn to make things from an actual cook? A woman who not only understood about living on a ranch, but also seemed nice.

Autumn could hardly wait.

WITH DINNER OVER and his belly pleasantly full, Cody settled back in his chair. "This was a good meal, Autumn. The hamburgers turned out great."

"Because you cooked them," she teased.

That was true. After showering and changing this afternoon, Cody had taken one look at the overabundance of coals piled in the pit of the grill, and had offered to teach her how to use the thing. Autumn had readily accepted.

His mouth quirked. "I didn't mind." He'd enjoyed showing her how to compress the meat so the patties didn't fall apart, and how to position them safely out of the way of any flames.

Thanks to the hours he'd put in baling hay, Cody's body had calmed down. He was in total control of his feelings and desires, and he felt very relaxed.

Autumn, too, seemed at ease. She didn't display any of the tension he'd expected after last night, which was both a surprise and a relief.

"You did the rest," he said. "She did a good job, huh?"

The boys seemed to be in mellow moods after taking

the day off. Discipline and routine were good for them, but they also needed time to just be kids.

"It wasn't half-bad," Ty said. "Those fries were totally raw."

Autumn looked alarmed. "They were?"

"*Raw* is slang for *delicious*," Cody translated.

She laughed in relief. "They were easy to fix. All I did was turn on the oven and bake them."

"Yeah, but you did it right."

"When someone says something kickin' to you, don't make excuses," Eric said, sounding like a hip version of Cody. "Say thank you."

Looking uncomfortable, Autumn rolled her eyes. "Thank you."

"It was good," Noah said. "But I wish we had rocky road ice cream for dessert. I'm tired of these cookies."

"I'll pick up a few gallons in the morning," Autumn said.

"You get the weekend off," Cody reminded her. "That's not necessary."

"I have to go into town anyway, to shop for my cooking lesson."

"That's great, but you could wait until next week."

"Tomorrow is best for Joan, and I'm so happy for her help that I don't mind at all."

"She'll do you well," he said, already anticipating the home-cooked meals to come.

"Which means I'll do well for you all."

Autumn's wide, easy smile rivaled any model's or actress's. How had he not noticed her years ago? Cody wondered.

Desire hit him hard.

Heat flared in her eyes, as if she sensed his hunger and shared it. A certain part of him started to rise. Silently willing his body to behave, he drained the last of his iced tea. Autumn brushed crumbs into her palm and emptied them on her plate.

He stood. "It's still your day off, guys, but let's get the table cleared and the dishwasher loaded. I'll take care of the rest."

"Then we're watching a movie, right?" Ty said.

"As long as we all get to bed at a decent hour. Don't forget, you have appointments with your therapists in the morning. Then after lunch we'll finish up the haying."

Whether because of the reminder of their therapy sessions or the prospect of the arduous chore tomorrow, no one looked happy. As soon as the boys had dealt with their dishes, they sauntered off.

Autumn started to rinse her plate, but Cody took it from her. "I'll take care of this. You're officially off until Monday."

"As I keep telling the boys, I really don't mind doing it."

Noting the stubborn glint in her eyes, Cody gave in. "We'll do what we did last night." Realizing how that sounded, he hurried to correct himself. "Finish the whole thing quickly, I mean."

They made a good team, Autumn washing the pots and pans and Cody drying.

"You mentioned therapy for the boys," she said over the hiss of the faucet. "Does it help?"

"What they discuss with their therapists is confidential, but it's bound to do them some good. Sure did for me."

She nodded, and loose strands of hair fluttered around her face like golden threads. "I have another question, about the garden," she said. "We have so much produce, more than we'll ever eat, and it'd be a shame if all that good food went to waste. Would you mind if I shared some with your crew?"

"That's a good idea," Cody said.

"Noah suggested it. He's a thoughtful kid."

She flashed another dazzling smile. Cody really liked that smile. He liked her, wanted her badly. Feelings he shouldn't be having.

Look away, a voice in his mind ordered, but God help him, he couldn't.

Autumn's cheeks flushed. She lowered her gaze and rinsed the dish sponge. "There's something else we need to discuss."

Cody figured she wanted to talk about what had happened last night. "I want to talk to you, too," he said.

But he wanted to kiss her more.

No way. He was *not* going to touch her. To avoid temptation, he left the remaining pots and pans in the dish rack and moved to the stove, a good five feet away.

With her back to him, Autumn wrung out the sponge and dried her hands. Her ponytail swished across her neck. Cody thought about brushing the hair aside and kissing her delicate nape. Then he'd work his way down to the crook of her shoulder. That little shiver would run through her. She'd turn around to face him, and kiss him as she had last night.

Get a grip, man.

As soon as they finished "the talk," he was out of there.

As if Autumn, too, needed her space, she leaned against the far counter and laced her fingers together at her waist.

"About last night…" she began, before hesistating.

Dishwater had dampened a large section of her white blouse, starting about rib-cage level and reaching up to her left nipple. The wet fabric was almost transparent, and Cody glimpsed the lace of her bra and the dark areola beneath. The sharp point of her nipple was clearly visible.

God Almighty.

His body went haywire. To hide the evidence of his desire, he sauntered as casually as possible to the table, pulled out a chair and straddled the seat backward.

He'd forgotten the topic of conversation. "What did you say you wanted to talk about?"

"Last night. We… I—I don't want you getting any ideas about me."

With her nipple all but screaming for attention, he had difficulty focusing. He nodded at her chest. "Uh, you splashed some water on your blouse."

She glanced down and her cheeks flushed crimson. Pivoting away, she dabbed at the splotch with a towel. *Lucky towel.* "Why didn't you say something?"

"I just did."

When she turned toward him again, she crossed her arms so that they covered her breasts.

Which helped, but not enough. In his mind, Cody still saw that nipple, teasing him like a siren's song.

He made sure his gaze stayed at eye level, which was no easy feat. "You were saying?"

"I'm not the kind of woman who jumps into bed with a man."

"If I thought you were, I'd have slept in your bed last night," he said. He couldn't hold back the hungry sweep of his gaze over her body.

Her eyes darkened, as if he'd touched her with his hands instead of his eyes. Suddenly he was rock hard.

This was getting beyond old, and was not at all what he needed right now. Where had his self-control gone?

He forced a neutral expression. "Go on."

"I work for you, and my job… I don't want…" She tightened her arms. "That is, I don't think we should kiss again."

Cody agreed. "You don't have to worry about your job, Autumn. The boys and I want you here. I'm not sorry I kissed you, but it won't happen again. Enjoy your weekend off, and I'll see you Monday."

Chapter Twelve

Relieved that the talk with Cody had gone well, Autumn slept soundly. Because she had Saturday off, she also slept in. By the time she'd showered and dressed, the boys and Cody were already gone. They hadn't made much noise that morning.

The house was quiet. Too quiet. Melancholy swept through her, but at least she had something fun to do this afternoon.

Tonight was a different story.

Maybe she'd borrow one of the Jeeps overnight, and stay at Heather's. When she'd called her mother and told her about Hope Ranch, Autumn had promised to pick up the mail once a week, so she needed to stop over there, anyway.

A night alone in the run-down duplex wasn't exactly her idea of fun, but it was better than hanging around the ranch, looking pathetically lonely. She had no idea what to do Sunday. It was too hot to be outside. Maybe she'd drive over to Elk Ridge, twenty-five miles away, and look for bargains at the department store there.

Autumn turned on the radio and sat down at the table in the main kitchen with her coffee and toast. She studied the grocery list Joan had dictated, adding ice cream and a few personal items, for which she needed her own money.

When she finished her breakfast, she returned to her apartment to get some cash and her purse. She pulled the dented can from the kitchen cabinet and brought it to the tiny café table she had yet to use.

The cap was on nice and tight, just as she'd left it, but the bills she kept so carefully organized were in disarray, several twenties facing backward, and a few tens mixed in with the fives and ones. Someone had been in her apartment!

Memories of Heather stealing from her piggy bank to buy cigarettes or takeout assaulted her.

Who had done this? Autumn always locked the door, and Cody had the only spare key. She knew he wouldn't come in without an invitation. It had to have been one or more of the boys, but how did they get in?

Sick at heart, she spilled the bills onto the table, then reorganized and carefully counted them. Two hundred and thirty dollars—nothing was missing.

Maybe she was mistaken—maybe no one had been in here.

The breath she'd held on to left her lungs in a relieved whoosh. She hadn't opened the can since filling it and sticking it in her suitcase the day she'd moved to the ranch. The bills must have shifted then. Which didn't seem possible, but had to be the only explanation.

Autumn extracted twenty dollars. Then she returned the remaining bills to the can and screwed the lid on tight. She returned the can to its place in the cabinet, and promptly dismissed her fears.

THE WEEKLY DRIVE to Flagg Clinic in Elk Ridge, where Cody took the boys for their therapy sessions, was roughly fifty miles round-trip. He'd quickly learned that the boys' moods were greatly affected by what happened during the sessions. Regardless, food usually helped. Unlike Saddlers Prairie, Elk Ridge offered a wide selection of restaurants, and he'd fallen into the habit of treating them to lunch before heading home.

After therapy, he eased the truck from its parking space and quickly took stock of the boys. Ty wasn't talking. He stared out the passenger window, his stiff posture signifying a rough session.

In the back, Noah shifted restlessly in his seat. Eric scowled and flexed his hands into fists, and sandwiched between them, Justin bowed his head so low that he appeared to curl into himself.

None of which boded well.

"Justin, it's your turn to choose the restaurant," Cody said. "What'll it be—Mexican, Italian, burgers and fries?"

When the boy didn't reply, Ty scowled at him over his shoulder. "Say something, ass wipe."

"Language," Cody warned.

Ty's scowl deepened. "What do you want to eat, Justin?"

The boy still didn't respond.

Ty snorted. "Fine, don't talk. How about we have Italian?"

"Everybody good with that?" Cody asked.

"Yep," Eric replied.

"Sure," Noah said.

Cody glanced in the rearview mirror. "If you want something different, Justin, say so now." The kid shrugged his shoulder. "I'll take that as a yes to Italian," Cody said. "Maybe I'll order the spaghetti today."

The subject of food got three of the four of them talking. By the time they ambled into the casual restaurant some minutes later, Ty, Eric and Noah were their usual selves. But Justin seemed the same as he'd been in the car.

The hostess led them to a booth and Cody slid in beside him.

"Look at *that,*" Eric murmured, jerking his chin toward a nearby booth, where two attractive teenage girls chattered and laughed over a pizza.

Everyone but Justin perked up. Ty broke into a cocky grin, Eric smoothed his hair and Noah straightened his shoulders.

"I'm gonna go wash up," Ty announced, glancing at the other booth.

Eric and Noah followed, the three of them all but swaggering past the two girls.

Justin kept his head down.

"You ought to check out those girls," Cody said. The boy gave an almost imperceptible shake of his head, and Cody added, "Interesting looks they're giving your foster brothers. I wonder what they're thinking?"

He expected a snarky comment, but Justin didn't react at all. Cody frowned. "You okay?"

"Not really."

"Want to talk about it?"

"Nope."

Cody squeezed one of the boy's thin shoulders. "If you change your mind, I'm here for you. Anytime, okay?"

"I won't."

Frustrated by his thwarted attempt to reach out, Cody searched his mind for something that might help. His thoughts went straight to Autumn. If she were with them, she'd likely say exactly what Justin needed to hear.

"Dinner last night was Autumn's best so far, but she's got a long way to go," he said, hoping the mention of her would help. "She's probably on her way to that cooking lesson right now. Think it'll do any good?"

"Shi— Man, I hope so." At last, Justin glanced at the girls in the booth. "They're okay, but too old for Noah and me. They look even older than Eric or Ty."

Cody hid his relief at the boy's response under a non-chalant shrug. "You're probably right, but it doesn't hurt to check them out."

Justin made a face. "Don't tell me *you're* interested."

"Hardly. I prefer women closer to my own age," he said, his thoughts on Autumn. Seven years younger was close enough.

"You like Autumn, huh?"

Either he was totally transparent or the kid was a mind reader. "No," Cody said. "I mean, yeah, I like her as a housekeeper."

"She's not your type?"

A week ago, he would have answered with a definite "no." But he couldn't straight-out lie… "It's not a good idea to get involved with someone who works for you," he said.

The other boys returned to the booth, and Cody changed the subject. "Who's up for a picnic and a swim tomorrow?"

AFTER LUNCH, ARMED with excess produce from the garden and supplies for her cooking lesson, Autumn stopped by the trailer area on the other side of the ranch, where a dozen units sat grouped around a small community yard. Most of the crew members who lived there were out working, but some of their wives were home. Autumn introduced herself and handed over boxes of zucchini, lettuce, beans and tomatoes. Everyone seemed pleased, and she drove away with a satisfied feeling.

A few minutes later, she pulled up in front of Joan and Doug's tidy little cottage. Colorful flowers lined the front walkway, and a vegetable garden very much like Cody's took up a good portion of the fenced side yard.

Balancing a heavy grocery bag on her hip, Autumn rang the doorbell. Moments later, a tall, slender woman opened the door. She had chin-length, dark brown hair and looked to be in her mid-thirties. "You must be Autumn," she said, offering a friendly smile. "Come on in. I just made a fresh pot of coffee."

As Joan led her toward the kitchen, Autumn glimpsed comfortable-looking living room furniture and cheerful prints on the walls.

The kitchen was only marginally bigger than the one in Autumn's apartment, but gingham curtains and colorful accessories gave the room a cozy, welcoming feeling. She felt instantly comfortable. "I like your place," she said.

"Thanks. How do you take your coffee?"

"With milk and sugar. Where should I put my groceries?"

"Anyplace on the counter is fine."

Autumn set her purse out of the way and brought her notebook and pen to the table. Joan handed her a mug of coffee and placed a tin of homemade oatmeal cookies between them. Joan was easy to talk to, and within minutes Autumn felt as if she'd known her forever.

"Doug seems like a really nice guy," Autumn said. "He's good-looking, too."

"I know." Smiling, Joan stared off into space, as if remembering that day. "I was helping with a cattle auction. At the time, he was working for Phil Covey, and the two of them were interested in buying new stock. Doug looked into my eyes and smiled, and then and there, I fell in love."

"That sounds so romantic," Autumn said. "How long did you know each other before you got married?"

"About a year. That was four years ago, about the time the doctors diagnosed Phil with pancreatic cancer." Joan sat back and shook her head. "He was a wonderful man, and I hate that he's gone. I'm really glad Cody is carrying on his legacy. He's a pretty amazing guy."

"He is," Autumn agreed, wondering what Joan would think if she knew what a great kisser he was. She considered confiding in her new friend, but not just yet—it seemed too personal. Besides, she and Cody weren't going to do that again.

"I can't imagine living with four teenage foster boys," Joan said. "You didn't say much about that the other day and I'm curious—what's it like?"

"Up and down. The boys can be belligerent and mistrustful, but other times, they're friendly and nice. Cody says they're going to test me a lot. They have a few times already."

She told Joan about the day the boys had invited themselves into her apartment, and about her cooking woes. "This is the hardest job I've ever had," she admitted.

"You've only been at it a week. It's bound to get better."

Autumn sure hoped so.

Joan hesitated and then, even though she and Autumn were alone in the house, she leaned forward and lowered her voice. "If I tell you a secret, will you promise to keep it to yourself?"

Autumn pantomimed zipping her lips shut.

"Doug and I are trying to get pregnant. I'm thirty-six and he's pushing forty. It's time."

Autumn envied her new friend for finding a decent man and building a life with him. "I hope it happens soon," she said.

"I'll keep you posted." Joan glanced at the wall clock. "I could sit here and talk all afternoon, but we really should get started. Otherwise we'll still be at it when Doug gets home. And I want my husband all to myself later this afternoon, so that we can work on that baby."

As Autumn washed her hands at the sink, she wondered if Cody wanted children of his own. Or were the four foster boys enough?

Joan loaned her a bib apron and handed over several recipes. "I copied these at work for you, so you won't need that notebook."

"Oh, but I will. If I take notes, I won't forget what to do."

"Trust me, it's easy. We'll start with the chocolate zucchini bars, and while they bake, we'll put the lasagna together and make the garlic bread."

"Making dinner while the dessert bakes—I like that," Autumn said. "Okay, tell me what to do."

Joan showed her how to assemble and operate a food processor, one of the mystery appliances in Cody's kitchen. Now she knew what it was and how to use it. In no time she'd finely diced the zucchini.

Joan was good at explaining things, and very patient. Autumn took advantage of her vast knowledge to ask cooking questions she'd gathered from other recipes.

Soon, wonderful aromas filled the air, making her mouth water. The room smelled just as she'd always dreamed a kitchen should. A mere two hours later, two large pans of chocolate zucchini bars sat on cooling racks, and the garlic bread and lasagna casseroles were wrapped and ready for the freezer.

Autumn made Joan sit and relax while she washed the dishes. "I can't begin to thank you for your help," she said.

"Maybe you can throw me a baby shower after I get pregnant."

By then, Autumn would be long gone from Hope Ranch. With any luck she'd have a new job, and a cottage or apartment somewhere in Saddlers Prairie. "I'll do that—wherever I am," she promised.

"What do you mean?"

"You haven't heard about my 'sixty-day sentence'?" Autumn said, referring to Judge Niemeyer's decision.

"Oh, that." Joan shrugged. "Ranching has a way of getting into your blood. You never know, you might end up liking the job and staying."

And continue to work side by side with Cody? Her attraction to her boss aside, cleaning the big house and keeping everyone fed was exhausting, and not exactly what Autumn pictured herself doing for the rest of her life. She wanted a *real* job, one where she worked in an office like Joan. There were office jobs in town where she hoped to find work.

Oblivious to her thoughts, Joan went on, "All I know is you sure impressed Doug and the crew when you made those extra sandwiches the other day. I'm sure Cody would be thrilled if you stayed on."

Autumn suspected he'd prefer someone more capable to run his house.

"This was fun," Joan said when the kitchen was once again tidy. "Let me know when you want to get together for another lesson."

"I will. Thank you."

Autumn left her place with a delicious-smelling meal and a budding friendship.

Chapter Thirteen

By the time Cody and the boys returned to the house Saturday afternoon, Autumn was gone. He found a note propped against the toaster, letting him know that she'd taken him up on his offer and borrowed a Jeep for the weekend. She wouldn't be back until late Sunday.

Knowing he wouldn't see her until Monday was a relief—or so he tried to tell himself. It wasn't. Who was she with? Judging by the way she'd kissed him the other night, Cody doubted she was with a man. And what if she was? The thought made him crazy.

But he had no claim on Autumn or who she spent her free time with, none at all.

He went to bed in a foul mood and woke up feeling just as wretched. Not even a refreshing Sunday swim with the boys helped.

As they polished off their picnic lunches under a lofty box elder at the edge of the river, Ty leaned back on his elbows and squinted at him. "You're in a crap mood."

Cody didn't argue. Wondering who Autumn was spending her time with was ruining his fun. "I didn't sleep well," he said. "I'll sleep better tonight."

Which was doubtful.

With the workday tomorrow starting bright and early, he figured he'd turn in early Sunday evening. Instead, he played with his iPad and waited up for her. When she still hadn't returned by ten he started getting anxious. What if she'd been in an accident? Or run off with some guy, as she had when she'd worked at Barb's?

She wouldn't take off with the Jeep, though. Too restless to sit any longer, he tossed the iPad aside and prowled around the house.

Just before eleven, he heard the rumble of the Jeep outside.

Autumn had come back.

Cody's shoulders sagged with relief. Calling himself an idiot for overreacting, and not about to let her know how stressed out he'd been, he took the stairs two at a time and ducked into his bedroom.

IT WAS GOOD to be back and to sleep in a decent bed, Autumn thought, after the alarm woke her early Monday morning. The Hide-A-Bed at Heather's was saggy and lumpy, making for a bad night's rest.

Eager to see Cody and the boys, she quickly showered and dressed before hurrying to the kitchen. They were all there at the table, eating breakfast. She'd missed them more than she'd ever imagined.

Two days away had felt like weeks, and she drank in the sight of them. Of Cody, especially. He made the kitchen seem somehow smaller and brighter. Freshly shaved, with his hair still wet from the shower, he looked particularly handsome this morning. His shoulders seemed impossibly broad in his sky-blue T-shirt, his arms muscular and tanned.

She didn't even try to curb her feelings. Her heart lifted with familiar warmth. "Good morning, everyone," she said.

"Morning," Noah replied. Ty and Eric mumbled hellos, and Justin dipped his chin.

Cody barely glanced at her. His brusque nod and hooded glance puzzled her. Was it her cutoffs? They *were* on the short side.

"How come you're dressed like that?" Noah asked.

"These are my cleaning clothes." The same clothes she'd worn to clean on Friday, but the boys had been gone then. "It's too hot to wear jeans." Self-conscious, she tugged on the frayed edges. "As soon as I finish your rooms, I'll change."

Now she had Cody's attention. His gaze traveled slowly from her head to her toes, warming her wherever it landed.

"Did you have a good weekend?" he asked.

His expression was shuttered and his tone casual, but underneath, Autumn sensed the hum of coiled tension.

"I had a great time with Joan." She smiled. "You're going to have a wonderful dinner tonight. The rest of the weekend was pretty low-key."

"Where were you?" Noah asked.

"I left a note on the toaster," she said as she poured herself a coffee. "Didn't you see it?"

"You didn't say where you were going," Cody replied lightly.

Spending the night at Heather's and all of Sunday in Elk Ridge had been lonely, although Autumn had found several summer tops and skirts on sale. She'd treated herself to dinner in Elk Ridge, followed by a stroll around town and a stop for an ice cream sundae, taking her time so as not to arrive at the ranch until late. "I went to Elk Ridge, but don't worry—I refilled the gas tank."

Cody nodded. He didn't seem to mind about the car, but something was definitely bothering him.

"Boyfriend?" he asked in the same nonchalant tone.

Autumn gaped at him. "How could I possibly have a boyfriend when I've barely been back in town three weeks?" *And after the way I kissed you?* she wanted to add. Because of the boys, she held her tongue.

Furious that Cody thought she would kiss him so passionately while she was involved with someone else— what kind of woman did he think she was?—she glared at him. "I made your lunches when I got home last night. They're in the refrigerator."

Taking her coffee mug, she left without giving Cody another glance and retreated to her apartment.

AUTUMN SAT AT the café table in her apartment until she heard the utility door click shut behind Cody and the boys. When she was sure they were gone, she stalked back to the kitchen—still fuming—and marched down the basement steps, where she retrieved the lasagna, garlic bread and zucchini bars from the big freezer. Back upstairs, she placed the food in the refrigerator.

Cody's assumption that she'd been with a man over the weekend grated on her. But the more she thought about his too casual tone and the tension emanating from him, the more she wondered if he was jealous.

No. He couldn't be.

Joan had confided in her. Now Autumn considered phoning Joan for advice. But she didn't know her well enough, and besides, her new friend was at work.

Anyway, she didn't have time to worry about Cody right now. The bedrooms and bathrooms weren't going to clean themselves. First on her list was Cody's suite.

The king-size bed was stripped, the bedspread folded neatly on an armchair and the dirty sheets nowhere in sight. He must've put them down the laundry chute. The men from Autumn's past would have expected her to take care of that, but Cody wasn't like them. He was considerate and thoughtful.

Which made him hard to stay mad at. Autumn fitted the fresh sheets in place, shook out the blanket and tucked in the edges. Clean pillowcase in hand, she grabbed a down pillow. Cody's familiar scent filled her nostrils—a mixture of shower soap and the essence that was uniquely his.

A wave of longing swept through her, but what was the point of wanting and dreaming about him, when she wasn't going near him ever again?

Especially now that he thought she had a boyfriend. Being mad helped. She fluffed the pillow and dropped it on the bed.

After dressing the other pillow, she added the bedspread, a dark brown, masculine thing.

There were several framed photos on the dresser. One was of Phil, his arm around a beaming woman who was obviously Sylvia. Another one showed the laughing couple and several youths in comical poses. But the one that really caught Autumn's attention showed Phil with Cody as a tall, gangly teenager. His surly expression reminded her of the boys.

He'd changed so much, and all for the better. Would they, too?

If anyone could help them grow into decent adults, Cody could. He was a good man, a special man, a man she couldn't stay mad at.

Too bad he was out of her league. Feeling melancholy, she hefted the tub of cleaning products and headed into the bathroom. With the exception of the skylight, the entire space was tiled in the prettiest terra-cotta squares she'd ever seen. Occasional hand-painted tiles added splashes of color. An open shower area big enough for two filled a good third of the space. There was also a large soaker tub, with spa jets.

It was a bathroom made for lovers.

A navy blue terry-cloth robe hung on a hook on the back of the door. Autumn didn't see any pajamas. Maybe Cody slept naked. She swallowed at the thought.

What was her problem? Cody may have kissed her, may have even seemed jealous this morning, but his interest wouldn't last. Someday he'd marry and share this suite with his wife, a woman with the class, beauty and intelligence he no doubt expected in a life partner.

Autumn didn't want to think about Cody's future wife, whoever she might be. Keeping her mind on her job, she finished the bathroom and then moved to the office.

When she was satisfied that the entire suite was spotless, she lugged the vacuum and cleaning supplies down the stairs.

After a short coffee break, she tackled the boys' bathroom. Then she made her way to the bedrooms. Cody was right—all four boys were reasonably tidy. Like him, they'd stripped their beds.

Posters of sports heroes and rock stars covered the walls of both bedrooms, but Autumn didn't see any personal photos.

As distant as she was from Heather, she knew her mother loved her in her own way. But Ty, Eric, Noah and Justin had no one but Cody to love them or cheer them on. Her heart ached for each of them.

By the time she finished, it was after two and she was famished. Changing out of her cleaning clothes could wait. She was eating a sandwich when she heard the door to the utility room open.

Not expecting anyone to be back for a while, she

frowned. She couldn't see who'd come in, but she heard the boys' footsteps thud across the floor. They didn't stop to remove their boots. Cody wouldn't like that, and neither did she. She was about to call out a reminder when Ty called out first.

"Autumn? Can you come in here?"

He didn't sound at all like his usual cocky self. He sounded young and scared.

"I'll be right there," she answered, dropping the remainder of her sandwich on her plate.

THE HEIFER LOWED steadily, her eyes wide and terrified.

If she kept jerking her head, she'd end up with a barb or three jammed into her pretty black hide. Cody swore under his breath. "Hold still, will you?"

It was another miserably hot afternoon, so hot he'd sent the boys home after lunch to swim and otherwise keep cool. He wanted nothing more than to strip off his clothes and jump into the river himself, and he'd considered doing exactly that. Then he and Doug had spotted the heifer tangled in the barbed wire fence.

"I'll hold her," the foreman said. "You cut her free."

As he spoke, the calf calmed.

"She likes your voice," Cody said. "Keep talking."

"Sure thing. Did Autumn tell you what she made for your dinner tonight?"

Cody shook his head. He'd been too keyed up this morning to ask. If that wasn't enough, she'd sashayed into the kitchen in a tight T-shirt and short cutoffs, all but killing him. His body had reacted predictably, which had pissed him off.

Then he'd asked who she'd been with and had made *her* mad. Women. The whole situation was one giant mess. He should probably apologize.

"You look like you're in pain," Doug said. "Cut yourself on that wire?"

"Nope." Cody almost wished he had. It might make him forget about her for a while. "Keep talking."

"Okay, let me tell you what you can look forward to for dinner." Doug launched into a vivid description of lasagna, garlic bread and chocolate zucchini bars that made Cody's mouth water and kept the heifer still.

By the time he cut her free and checked her over to make sure she was okay, his belly was clamoring for dinner, which wasn't for hours yet.

Chapter Fourteen

The boys gathered around the utility room sink, where Justin clutched a bloody towel to his hand.

So much blood. Autumn gasped. "What happened? Where's Cody?"

"It's really hot outside today," Eric said. "He said we could relax after we took care of our horses."

Ty nodded. "We were gonna go swimming. Then..." He cast a worried glance at Justin.

"Justin's cut bad," Noah said, looking like a frightened little boy.

Autumn was frightened, too. The towel was saturated. "You need a fresh towel." She pawed through the clean cloths in the rag bin and handed him a replacement.

He dropped the bloody towel into the sink, revealing a gaping wound on his left palm.

Autumn felt sick to her stomach. "You need to see a doctor right away," she said. Saddlers Prairie Medical Clinic was the closest facility. "Press hard against the cut and hold your hand up, like this, to slow the bleeding."

Pale and swallowing, Justin did as he was told. "Will you drive me?" he asked in a small, scared voice.

"Of course—just let me call Cody first."

She hurried to the kitchen phone, the boys behind her. Justin collapsed in a chair at the table.

Cody answered on the third ring. "Yeah?"

He sounded wary, probably because she'd been angry with him this morning. Which he'd deserved, but for now she was over it.

"Justin…he… Here, he'll tell you." She held the phone to the boy's ear.

"I cut myself," he said simply. "Autumn's gonna drive me to the doctor's office." He listened for a moment. "I got through brushing and watering Paint before Ty and the other guys. They said to wait, so I started cutting on a piece of wood. The knife slipped and…" The words trailed off, Justin's throat working as if fighting tears. "I'm sorry, Cody."

He listened some more. Then, with a guilty expression, handed the phone to Autumn. "He wants to talk to you again."

"Is it that bad?" Cody asked.

She glanced at the bloodied rag and looked away. "I'm afraid so."

"Then what are you waiting for? I'll call ahead and let Dr. Mark know you're coming, and I'll meet you at the clinic."

"You don't have to do that, Cody. I can handle this."

"Maybe I want to. Justin needs me, and I want to be there for him."

More impressed with him than ever, Autumn hung up and turned to Justin. "Cody will meet us at the clinic. Let's go."

"What about the rest of us?" Ty asked.

"You stay here and keep an eye on things. As soon as we see the doctor, either Cody or I will call you."

WORKING HARD TO appear calm, Autumn gripped the steering wheel. "Does it hurt?"

"A little."

Justin's ashen skin and pinched expression belied his words. He was in pain.

The clinic was still some seven miles away. Except for the Jeep, the highway was empty, and Autumn was strongly tempted to push the accelerator to the floor. But experience had taught her better, and she stifled the urge and stayed within the speed limit.

"Keep that hand up," she said. "If it were me, I'd be crying up a storm. You're so brave."

"Crying's for girls and sissies."

"Who told you that?"

"My old man."

"It's okay for guys to cry," she said.

"Yeah, right." Justin eyed her skeptically.

"Guys are allowed to cry anytime, but especially when something sad happens. Like when a person they love dies."

"You mean like Cody's foster dad, Phil?"

"That's right."

"Did Cody cry?"

"I wasn't here then, but I wouldn't be surprised if he did. I'm sure he'll tell you if you ask him."

Justin didn't reply. His whole body radiated tension, and Autumn suspected the pain was severe.

"You told Cody you were cutting wood with a knife," she said, hoping that talking would take his mind off his injury. "What exactly were you doing?"

"Zeke's always whittling stuff on his break. The other day, he made a whistle for his son. I saw one of his special knives on the table in the barn and decided to make myself a whistle just like it." Justin bit his lip. "Instead, I cut the bejesus out of my hand."

He certainly had. "Have you ever whittled before?"

The boy shook his head. "But it didn't look too hard. I thought I could figure out how to do it."

"Sounds like me with cooking. Sometimes teaching yourself doesn't work out so well, huh?" Hoping to relax him a little, she smiled.

To her dismay, he tensed up even more.

"Joan's teaching me to cook," she hurriedly added. "I think you'll like the meal we made for dinner tonight. Maybe Zeke will teach you to whittle."

"I'm not good at learning stuff from other people."

He sounded just like Autumn had at his age. Her heart went out to him. "Maybe you haven't had the right teacher," she said. "Mrs. Dawson, who'll be your teacher when you start school in a few weeks, is really great."

"I hate school."

Autumn understood that, too, though she'd enjoyed attending the one-room school in Saddlers Prairie, where everyone had helped each other. High school had been a different story. "I know exactly how you feel, Justin, but I promise you'll like the school here. We should be at the clinic soon, by the way."

"Do you think I'll need stitches?" he asked, his face etched with anxiety.

"If you do, Dr. Mark will take good care of you." Autumn had met the new doctor once, on the day when he'd saved the lives of two people. Florence Jones had experienced a stroke while driving on the highway, and hours later her doctor, Dr. Tom, had suffered a major heart attack. A few days later, Autumn had run off with Teddy. She hadn't seen Dr. Mark since, but had heard that everyone in town liked him.

"Cody will probably arrive soon after we do," she added.

Instead of looking relieved, Justin cringed. "He's gonna kill me."

Puzzled, Autumn frowned. "Why would you say that, Justin? Did he sound angry on the phone?"

"No, but that doesn't mean anything. My old man used to act nice when other people were around, too. But as soon as we were alone…" The boy's shudder spoke volumes.

"You know Cody isn't like that," she said.

"Yeah, but I messed up."

"I talked to him on the phone before and after you did, remember? Trust me, he's a lot more worried than angry."

"My old man used to beat me if I made a mistake."

Autumn was appalled. "He was wrong to do that."

"That's what Cody says."

And yet Justin still worried that Cody, decent and caring as he was, might physically hurt him. It didn't make sense, and Cody needed to know. "Is that why you ran away from home?" she asked.

Justin shook his head. "My dad went to jail because of his bad temper. My mom got a new boyfriend and didn't want me around no more, so I took off. She doesn't want me back."

What kind of mother chose a boyfriend over her own son? No wonder Justin had run away. "You have a home here now, with Cody," Autumn said, burning with anger. "*He* wants you." The yearning on the boy's face broke her heart. "I think you're a pretty cool kid," she added.

He didn't react to her compliment, although his shoulders seemed a little less rigid. Changing the subject to a more pleasant topic, she told him about the Saddlers Prairie Medical Clinic. "Only two people work at the facility—Stacy manages the office and her husband, Dr. Mark, treats the patients." Autumn had met Stacy when she'd gone in for a prescription for birth control pills. She hadn't seen her since she'd been back, and still couldn't believe Stacy had married the handsome doctor, who was supposedly only in Saddlers Prairie temporarily and eager to start a new job at a fancy clinic in L.A. She'd heard that he'd fallen for Stacy before he left town, and after a few months at his new job, he'd come back to run the clinic and marry her.

"We don't even need an appointment here," Autumn told Justin.

"Like at the E.R.?"

"It's nothing like that. This clinic is much smaller and friendlier."

She was still wearing her T-shirt and raggedy cutoffs, and wished she'd taken the time to change before lunch.

But she couldn't worry about that now. As the clinic came into view, she slowed and signaled. "Hold on tight, Justin," she said. "We're almost there."

"AUTUMN KNOWLES! IT'S good to see you," Stacy said, as friendly as ever. "I heard you were back in town."

Stacy had always been pretty, but now her eyes were alight with an extra sparkle. "You look great. Congrats on your marriage," Autumn told her.

"Thanks." Stacy smiled at her, before she turned to the boy. "You must be Justin. Cody called a little while ago and let us know you were coming. It's nice to finally meet one of his boys." She glanced at the bloody rag around Justin's hand. "I'm just sorry you had to hurt yourself in order to visit us."

His ears reddened. By all appearances he was tough and hard, but Autumn knew that hiding inside that shell was a shy boy who wanted desperately to be loved.

"You're lucky we're having a slow afternoon," Stacy

went on. "You won't have to wait long. Why don't you sit down while I buzz Dr. Mark."

She pressed a button on the phone and spoke into the receiver. Moments later, the handsome doctor cruised into the waiting area.

"Hello, Justin, I'm Dr. Mark." He squinted at the towel. "What happened to that hand?"

Justin glanced at Autumn, indicating that he wanted her to explain. "Hi, Dr. Mark. I'm Autumn Knowles, the housekeeper at Hope Ranch. Justin cut himself with a whittling knife."

"I see. Come on back to my office, Justin, and let me take a look at that."

"Do you want me to come with you?" Autumn asked.

"Whatever," the boy muttered. He'd slipped back into his usual surly mode, but now that she knew him better, she understood that he wanted her there.

Once inside, Dr. Mark gestured for Justin to sit on the exam table. Not wanting to be in the way, Autumn stood back.

"So, you cut yourself." The doctor deftly removed the sodden towel. "That's a deep one," he said. "You were right to come here. I'm going to give you a shot to numb the wound so that I can clean it."

"Will it hurt?"

"I won't lie to you, the shot packs a mean sting. But I'll bet you're brave enough to handle it."

Justin's narrow shoulders straightened. "I am."

"If you need a hand to hold, I'm here," Autumn said.

"I'm okay," he insisted, but when the needle slid into his palm, he grabbed on to her and squeezed so hard her fingers throbbed.

"Good job, Justin." Dr. Mark set the syringe aside, and Justin released his death grip on Autumn's hand.

"It'll take a minute to kick in. Do you know when you had your last tetanus shot?"

The boy shook his head.

"Cody's on his way," Autumn said. "He'll probably know."

The doctor nodded and gently touched an uninjured part of the boy's palm. "Do you feel this?"

"No, and it doesn't hurt anymore."

"That's good. I'm going to clean the wound now."

As he set to work, Justin compressed his lips so hard they almost disappeared.

Dr. Mark paused. "You sure it doesn't hurt?"

"I'm sure. Am I gonna get stitches?"

"Definitely."

"A lot of them?"

"From the length of this gash, I'd say about seven or eight. What about your other shots? Do you know if you're up-to-date?" he asked as he gathered up the suturing supplies.

"I had some, but I'm not sure whi—"

Someone knocked on the door, cutting him off. An instant later it swung open, and Cody entered the room.

CODY WAS SWEATY and dirty and needed a shower, but he'd wanted to get to the clinic fast. He'd asked Ty to take care of Diablo, and had come straight here. He nodded at Autumn. Her ponytail hung askew, and she was still wearing the short cutoffs and tight T-shirt she'd had on earlier. Neither of them had taken the time to clean up.

She looked relieved to see him. "You made it," she said, before returning her attention to Justin.

The boy seemed tense. Cody figured he would be, too, if some doctor was stitching his skin together.

Dr. Mark glanced up at him and nodded.

"Hey, buddy," Cody said, joining Autumn near the exam table. "How's it going?"

"Not too bad."

Justin put on a brave front, but anyone could see the kid was scared stiff.

Something about Autumn's gaze, and the way she hovered close enough to Justin to reach him if he needed her, reminded Cody of a mother bear. She seemed to genuinely care about the boy.

"Will Justin be okay, Dr. Mark?" he asked.

"Once the stitches are out, he'll be as good as new. He isn't sure whether he's up-to-date on his shots. Do you have that information?"

"I'd have to check the records, which are at the house. Can I get back to you on that?"

"Fax them over anytime. To be on the safe side, I'll give him a tetanus shot today," Dr. Mark said as he completed another stitch. "You'll want to schedule an appointment before school starts, for a physical and any other shots he needs."

"What do I need a physical for?" Justin grumbled.

"I like to schedule one every year, just to make sure you're growing as you should."

"It's just a checkup, Justin. No big deal," Cody said.

Despite his reassurance, the boy looked wary. "If I have to get one, so should Noah and Ty and Eric."

Dr. Mark nodded. "They should come in, too. I'll ask Stacy to set it up. Okay, all done. Take a look." He showed the boy the neat row of stitches closing the wound.

Justin studied his palm. "Did I get seven stitches or eight?"

"Eight."

"Wow. Wait'll the rest of the guys see this."

"It's something, all right. In about ten days the stitches

should start to dissolve, so you won't have to come back and have them removed. In the meantime, keep that hand clean and dry." Using a Q-tip, Dr. Mark spread ointment over the wound. Then he rolled a gauze bandage around Justin's hand and secured it with a silver clip.

"When can I go swimming?" the boy asked.

"Wait at least a week." Mark handed Cody the tube of ointment. "Apply this twice a day, when you change the bandage. If the skin looks red or Justin's hand swells, or you notice any red streaks, bring him back right away."

"Thanks, Dr. Mark," Cody said.

"I'm happy I could help. It was nice meeting you, Justin. Tell your friends that I look forward to meeting them, too."

The boy nodded. "Is there a bathroom here?"

"Down the hall and to your left."

"Soon as this weather cools down, let's go hiking again," Dr. Mark said as Justin disappeared.

Cody hadn't enjoyed a hike with the doc in at least a year. "Sure, if you don't mind the boys coming along."

"The more, the merrier. Good to see you again, Autumn," Dr. Mark said, and then he left the room—leaving Cody and Autumn alone.

Chapter Fifteen

"I'm glad that's over with," Cody told Autumn. "Thanks for getting Justin here."

"I didn't have much choice, he was bleeding so badly. We were both a little scared." She shuddered. "I'm just relieved that he's going to be okay."

An awkward silence descended. A silence that had nothing to do with Justin and everything to do with what had happened that morning.

With her lips pursed and her arms crossed, Cody figured she was still miffed at him. Unsure how to smooth things out, he said nothing.

After a few tense seconds, she huffed and turned toward the door. He couldn't let her walk away, not like this. "Hold on," he said.

"Yes?" she said, her eyebrows raised.

He pushed the door closed so that they wouldn't be overhead. "You're still mad at me, and I don't like it."

"You're darn right I am. Assuming I have a boyfriend, when you and I… Do you really think I'd have kissed you if I was involved with someone?"

"You spent the night someplace, and I know your mom's out of town," he said, scrubbing the back of his neck.

"So you assumed I was with some other guy." Hurt

flashed in her eyes and her chin notched up. "You must not think much of me."

Cody wanted to cup her stubborn chin and kiss the hurt and anger right out of her. But they'd agreed not to do that again. "I think the exact opposite," he said, picking up the salve and bandages to keep from reaching for her. "The more I get to know you, the more I respect you. The idea of you with someone else… I didn't like it."

Damn. He hadn't meant to admit that.

"Really?" Her expression softened.

Mercy, she was beautiful. Swallowing, he tightened his grip on the medical supplies.

"Heather *is* gone, but I stayed at her place," Autumn said. "I spent Sunday in Elk Ridge because I felt funny staying at the ranch on my weekend off."

Cody frowned. "Why would you feel that way? The ranch is your home."

Instead of answering, she tugged at the ragged ends of her cutoffs.

"The boys and I went swimming and had a picnic on Sunday," he said. "You could've joined us."

"I don't want to intrude on your time with them."

"We get plenty of time together," he countered. "Trust me, they'd tell you if they didn't want you along."

"No doubt."

She smiled, and Cody relaxed. "You're not mad anymore?"

Autumn shook her head. "But next time you have questions about who I'm with or what I'm doing, just ask."

"I will." Justin was taking his sweet time. "Tell me again how Justin cut himself."

"I guess Zeke left one of his knives on the table in the barn, and Justin decided to teach himself how to whittle."

Cody swore. "The other afternoon, Zeke spent a good thirty minutes sharpening those things. He should've put them away. Because he didn't, we had a senseless accident."

"Well, what's done is done. I'm sure next time he'll be more careful where he leaves them."

Probably, but Cody wasn't ready to drop the matter. Now that he knew Justin was going to be okay, feelings he'd stifled rose to the surface. "You don't touch things that aren't yours without asking permission. That's how Justin got into so much trouble and ended up with me—he stole from his mom. He's lucky she dropped the charges." Exasperated, Cody shook his head. "We've been over that half a dozen times. Why in hell doesn't he listen?"

Autumn's eyes widened. "You *are* angry."

What did she mean by that? "Damn straight, I am—at both him and Zeke. Justin's lucky—his injury could've been much worse. I didn't want to say anything while he got his stitches, but you'd better believe he and Zeke will both hear about this." Cody's voice had risen, but when he thought about what might have happened…

"Calm down, okay? He already feels bad enough. He just wanted to try his hand at whittling. I told him that next time he should ask Zeke for lessons."

Cody sucked in a breath and reined in his frustration. "That's not a bad idea."

"What did he take from his mom?"

"All the money in her wallet, and then he ran away."

"She didn't want him anymore, Cody. You can't blame him for leaving or for taking that money. He needed it to buy food for himself."

"He told you about his mom?"

Autumn nodded. "He also told me that his father used to beat him whenever he made a mistake."

"He's really starting to trust you. Did he mention that things were especially bad when his father was high on meth?"

"I didn't know about the drugs." She chafed her arms as if suddenly chilled. "Justin told me he was worried you'd be angry at him. He's afraid you'll beat him, too."

The words hit him like a sucker punch to the gut. Cody winced. "I've been nothing but kind to that kid. Sure, I raise my voice now and then, when necessary, but that's it. How could he possibly think I'd ever lay a hand on him?"

"That's exactly what I said. Eventually, he'll come to believe it."

Cody was beginning to wonder. Discouraged, he shook his head. "What am I supposed to do?"

"Maybe you and Justin can sit down and talk this through."

Couldn't hurt, he decided, as they started toward the waiting room.

"I'd better call the boys and let them know about Justin," Autumn said. "Then I'll head back to the house and heat up tonight's dinner. I think you're going to like this meal."

Justin trudged toward them, his shoulders slumped and his uninjured hand shoved into his pocket.

"Does your cut hurt?" Autumn asked. She brushed Justin's long hair out of his eyes—a tender gesture he would never normally have tolerated.

The boy shook his head. "It's still numb from the shot."

Soon his palm would hurt like a son of a bitch, and they all knew it.

"You look like you just ran out of steam," Cody said.

"I'm, like, really tired."

"I'll bet. You've had a big shock this afternoon. You should rest before dinner." He clapped his hand on Justin's shoulder. "Let's go home."

SEATED AT THE dinner table between Justin and Noah, Autumn held her breath and waited for the verdict. No one was talking, which made her nervous. On the other hand, they were all gobbling up the lasagna and garlic bread. That was a good sign, right?

Finally, Cody set down his fork and wiped his mouth. "This lasagna is delicious—every bit as good as Doug promised."

The boys nodded but didn't comment. They were too busy wolfing down their food. Even Justin, still pale from this afternoon's fiasco, was eating with gusto.

With pride swelling in her chest, Autumn glanced at her hands. "Joan supervised while I made it. She should really get the credit."

"Autumn," Eric said with exaggerated impatience, "you're supposed to say—"

"Thank you." She flashed him a smile. "Okay?"

"See how easy that was?" Cody winked and then glanced around the table. "Tell her what you think of the food."

"You really scored," Justin said. He even smiled before turning back to his plate.

"This is raw," Ty agreed.

His mouth full, Noah gave an enthusiastic nod.

"It's awesome." Eric cocked his eyebrow.

"Thank you, Eric. Thank you all," she murmured, filled with warmth.

"No, thank *you*." Cody gave her a tender, utterly irresistible look that made her feel as if her heart had expanded to fill her chest. In the hours since the accident, her feelings toward him had changed. Especially after Cody had admitted that he didn't want her to be with anyone else. Never mind that *he* wasn't going to be with her, either. She understood—she felt the same way about him.

Better still, he *respected* her—and it had been a long time since she'd felt respected by a man.

She wanted to melt. She liked this man too much for her own good.

"Who wants a chocolate zucchini bar?" she asked, pushing her chair back.

Ty rubbed his hands together. "Bring them on!"

THE HOT SPELL of the past couple of weeks had broken all records. In an effort to avoid heatstroke, Cody and his crew drank gallons of water and made sure to do most of their outside chores before 10:00 a.m. or after 6:00 p.m. The rest of the day they worked in the barn or other outbuildings fitted with fans. Cody limited the boys' chores to tending the garden and seeing to the horses.

Pleased with the extra time to themselves, Ty, Eric and Noah spent long afternoons swimming in the river, while Justin stayed back at the house.

On Wednesday, Cody decided to join the boys for a swim. Later, he returned to the house alone, since the boys weren't ready to leave yet. When he entered the kitchen, Justin and Autumn were at the table, eating a snack.

"Hey," he said, ducking into the fridge for the pitcher of iced tea.

Autumn's whole face brightened as if she was glad to see him. "Did you have a good time?"

It'd been some time since a woman's eyes had lit up at

the sight of him, and Cody's heart thudded in his chest. "The water's almost too warm, but it felt good," he said. "The boys are still swimming. Are those more zucchini bars? I thought we polished them off last night."

"Autumn made another batch this morning. These are even better than before," Justin declared.

Cody needed a shower, but it could wait. He helped himself to a thick slice, wolfing it down. "You're right. You could win a prize with this stuff."

Autumn beamed. Confidence suited her, brightened her eyes, tilted the corners of her mouth. She was beautiful, and so damn desirable. The hunger that was always with him flared up, and he wanted her more than ever.

Not sure he could control his feelings, he grabbed his glass of iced tea. "I'll be upstairs."

When he'd showered, he headed down again, to find that Justin and Autumn were still in the kitchen. Their voices carried easily in the otherwise quiet house. Standing out of sight in the hallway, Cody eavesdropped shamelessly.

"There's only half a pan left," Autumn was saying.

"That won't be enough for dessert tonight," Justin said. "Teach me how, and I'll make more."

Cody couldn't believe his ears. Had Justin just offered to make *dessert?*

"Are you sure you want to learn from me?" she asked.

"You said that if I had the right teacher, I could learn." *When had they discussed that?*

"What about your hand?" she asked.

"I'll be careful. I'll wear a latex glove, like when I shower."

The kid sounded painfully eager. No doubt about it, he was growing more attached to Autumn every day. He was in a fragile place, and Cody hoped to God she didn't let him down. That could set him back months. After dinner, he'd take her aside and make sure she understood.

"Okay," she said. "We have enough time, so let's do it. Joan started by going over the recipe with me, so that's what we'll do."

Cody peeked around the doorway to watch the two of them. Sitting side by side, bent over the recipe, they didn't see him. Autumn's dishwater-blond ponytail and pale complexion contrasted sharply with Justin's dark brown hair and mocha skin.

She reviewed the directions, explaining the various steps with humor and a touch of self-deprecation that charmed Cody.

By the looks of it, he wasn't the only one who was charmed. Shooting her worshipful glances, Justin listened, asked the occasional question and laughed. *Laughed.*

Cody counted his blessings that Autumn had come to the ranch. She might not realize it, but she was a miracle worker.

"*You* MADE THIS?" Noah gaped at Justin. "But it tastes so good."

Wearing a self-satisfied expression Cody had never seen, Justin nodded. "Autumn taught me."

"Cool, man," Ty said, looking impressed.

"You did great, Justin," Cody added.

The boy puffed up his chest. "I might be a chef someday."

Thinking about his future—another first. Tonight was full of positive surprises. Cody caught Autumn's eye and nodded in gratitude. Her smile telegraphed her joy. Once again his body stirred.

"I thought you wanted to be a whittler," Noah said.

"I'd rather learn to cook."

"You can do both," Autumn said. "When you do become a chef, I'll eat your food anytime."

Justin gave her a goofy, love-struck look. He was totally smitten with her.

But then, they all were.

Feelings Cody wasn't ready to explore settled in his chest. He told himself he was pleased about her progress with the boys, but it was so much more than that.

Ty and Eric had kitchen duty, and Justin and Noah headed for the great room. Before Autumn could offer to help with the dishes, Cody gestured for her to follow him to the utility room.

"What is it?" she asked.

He stepped close and lowered his voice so that he could keep the conversation between the two of them. The smell of lilacs teased his senses. "When I finish the evening chores and the boys turn in for the night, we should talk about Justin," he said.

She gave him a questioning look. "Am I doing something wrong?"

"It's nothing like that, but I'd rather discuss it later."

Looking anxious, she nodded.

Wanting to reassure her, Cody touched her shoulder. "I promise, it's fine."

She sucked in a breath.

"Please don't worry." He traced the curve of her shoulder with his fingers. Her skin was so soft.

Her wary eyes softened and lost focus, and her pupils enlarged in a wordless plea.

Cody forgot that he wasn't going to kiss her again. He was leaning down to taste her when laughter floated from the kitchen. At the same instant, he and Autumn jerked away from each other.

Cheeks flushed, she smoothed her blouse. "When you're ready to talk, I'll be in my apartment."

If he were smart, he'd talk to her in the morning, after he corralled his feelings. Instead he nodded, already anticipating the night ahead.

Chapter Sixteen

Cody had almost kissed Autumn in the utility room, and she had almost let him.

Her mind in turmoil and her heart racing, she sat on the sofa in her living room, attempting to watch TV while she waited for Cody.

He'd said he wanted to talk about Justin, but his eyes had told a different story.

Their agreement to stay away from each other then had been made for all the right reasons, and Cody had seemed as determined to keep that agreement as she was.

Yet tonight… One gentle touch, one yearning look from him and her resolve had crumbled like dust. She wasn't sure she had the strength to resist him, and she wasn't sure she wanted to.

Giving up on TV, she jumped up and paced to the window. She stared out at the growing dusk, watching as the sky and the fields faded into darkness.

She shouldn't see him tonight, not until she pulled herself together. When he showed up, she'd tell him she felt sick, and postpone their talk until tomorrow.

The soft knock on her door startled her. Her stomach lurched.

Afraid to let Cody into the apartment, fearing she might do something reckless, she poked her head out and opened her mouth to tell him she wasn't feeling well. The warmth in his smile broadsided her, and the words died in her throat.

"It's a beautiful night," he said. "Let's take a walk."

That sounded safe enough, she decided. There was plenty of room outside to keep a safe distance from him.

They moved silently through the utility room and out the side door. The air had cooled to a bearable temperature, aided by a gentle breeze. A sliver of moon hung overhead, and a thousand stars spilled across the sky.

Accompanied by a symphony of chirping crickets, Cody led Autumn past the barn. At first she couldn't see where she was going. She stumbled a few times before her eyes adjusted to the dark.

She had no idea where they were going, but as long as they kept moving, she was safe. From Cody. From herself.

He didn't speak until they neared a large tree about a hundred yards beyond the barn. He gestured to a rope swing hanging from a thick, leafy branch.

"Phil brought me here shortly after he took me in," he said.

"Did you used to come out here a lot?"

"Not at first. I thought I was too old and too tough for a swing, but when I needed to think, this is where I came. Something about the back and forth rhythm helped my mind work."

"It's been years since I sat on a swing," Autumn said. "Would you mind if I tried it?"

"Be my guest."

Grasping the ropes, she hoisted herself into the wooden seat, which was wide enough for someone twice her size.

Cody stepped behind her and pushed her, his hands warm between her shoulder blades.

The rush of air and the feeling that she was flying were

wonderful, and she forgot all her worries. Cody pushed her higher, and she laughed. "This is awesome! The boys have got to try this."

"I've suggested it several times, but they think they're too cool."

Autumn imagined Justin soaring high, the wind billowing under his T-shirt. If he felt half as exhilarated as she did right now, he needed to come out here.

"Justin has a big crush on you," Cody said.

"I wouldn't call it a crush," she said as she pumped her legs. "We have gotten closer, though. It's nice that he's let his guard down around me."

"I don't want him getting hurt."

Autumn frowned as she sailed past him. "Neither do I."

"Are you planning to keep in touch after you leave?"

She hadn't thought that far ahead. "I could," she said, observing the moon through the thick leaves. "If you want."

Cody stepped in front of her and grasped the ropes, bringing the swing to a stop. "Oh, I want."

Clasping her around the waist, he set her on her feet. Instead of letting her go, he moved even closer. In the moonlight, his eyes glittered with unmistakable heat.

Don't do it! a voice in Autumn's head silently shouted.

She made a feeble attempt to back away, but Cody anchored her where she was.

"I promised not to kiss you again, Autumn, and I'm about to break my word."

She wrapped her arms around his neck.

AUTUMN PRESSED AGAINST him, all softness and warmth. She tasted as sweet as Cody remembered, her lips eager and willing.

Need roared through him, and he deepened the kiss, his tongue tangling wildly with hers.

He ran his palms up her rib cage, skimming the sides of her breasts, sliding his fingers toward her nipples.

She went still. Reluctantly, he lowered his hands.

"Don't stop," she whispered, tugging them back.

Her breasts filled his palms and then some. Moaning softly, she pressed herself into his cupped hands. Her passion burned into him until he wasn't sure he could stand much longer.

Still kissing her, Cody backed toward the tree. When he bumped into the trunk, he slid to the ground, bringing her with him. The rough bark scraped his back, but he was focused on the woman in his arms. On his lap, her soft bottom teasing his erection.

"Now, where were we?" he said, drawing his index finger across her nipple. Instantly, it sharpened to a hard point.

Autumn sucked in a breath and dropped her head to his shoulder. Her face a mask of passion, she squirmed against him. His body hardened painfully.

But this was about her.

He pulled away and tugged on the hem of her top. A moment later, it lay discarded on the ground. She wore a stretchy white sports bra that almost glowed in the faint moonlight. Her nipples stood taught and aroused against the fabric.

Blood roared in Cody's ears. Desperate to taste her, he suckled her through the bra.

She arched her back, and sweet sounds escaped from her throat.

Cody paused, grinning. "You like this."

"Yes." She tangled her hands in his hair and urged him close again.

He couldn't remember ever being this turned on, and her sounds of pleasure only increased his arousal. His erection throbbed, demanding release. He wanted to lay her down and slide into her slick heat.

He was about to do just that when Autumn pushed him away. "We'd better stop."

Breathing heavily, he retrieved her top. She silently tugged it over her head and smoothed the hem over her stomach, then retied her ponytail.

Unable to keep from touching her, he held her hand on the walk back. Neither of them spoke. He let go of her before they reached the door—just in case one of the boys was up.

The house was dark and as quiet as when they'd left.

Cody walked her through the alcove. "'Night."

"Good night, Cody." She touched his face, then slipped through her apartment door.

AT NOON ON Saturday, Autumn met Sherry at the Burger Palace for lunch. After ordering, they slid into a booth.

Sherry started twirling a lock of hair around her finger, which meant she was upset.

"Did you and Shawn have a fight?" Autumn asked.

She gave a solemn nod. "He wants to move in together, but I won't without a ring."

"Good for you," Autumn said, admiring her friend for being so smart.

"I guess." Propping her head in her hand, Sherry sighed. "We were supposed to go out tonight, but he's so angry, we probably won't."

"You'll make up. If he loves you, he'll come around." At least that was what Autumn had always been told. No man had every truly loved her, so she didn't really know.

"I hope so." Her friend straightened. "But I don't want

to talk about my problems, I want to hear about you. We haven't talked in a while. What's been happening down at Hope Ranch?"

Autumn fiddled with her straw, wanting to explain the turn her relationship with Cody had taken, but not sure she could. By day they were friendly with each other as usual, but that was it. But when the boys went to sleep and they were alone, they couldn't keep their hands off each other.

"Order's up," a teenage boy called out.

"I'll get it," Sherry said. "After your week, you need to relax."

Her friend had no idea. As Sherry headed for the counter, Autumn thought dreamily about the past three nights. Last night, like the two nights before, she and Cody had slipped outside, where they wouldn't be seen or heard, and headed again for the swing.

On the way, they'd stopped at the barn to grab an old quilt, which they'd spread on the ground under the canopy of leaves. Sheltered by the darkness and the tree, they'd shared delicious kisses and caresses that had left Autumn yearning for more.

Unlike the previous Saturday, tonight she would stay at the ranch. Reckless and dangerous as those stolen hours with Cody were, she couldn't seem to stop herself. She shivered with anticipation, thinking of the evening to come.

Sherry returned to the table with a tray. "I'm starving," she said, handing Autumn her food. After a few bites, she asked, "How's Justin doing?"

"His hand is healing nicely. He still can't help with the heavy chores, which bothers him, but he's been hanging around the house, keeping me company and helping with some of the lighter cleaning jobs. We're also learning how to cook together. Justin has never shown an interest in anything before, so Cody's really pleased."

Sherry's eyebrows rose. "That moody kid who hardly talks wants to learn how to cook?"

Autumn shrugged. "He was bored the other day, and we needed dessert, so I let him help me make chocolate zucchini bars. Thanks to the cooking lesson I got from my new friend, Joan, they turned out great. His foster brothers were impressed, and now he's talking about being a chef someday. Pretty cool, huh?"

Still thinking about the boy, Autumn bit into her chicken burger. The more time she spent with him, the more she was getting to see the real Justin.

She didn't mind that he was growing attached to her. She genuinely liked him, too. She probably *would* keep in touch with all the boys, and visit from time to time.

"He's getting antsy, though," she went on. "Yesterday, he actually pleaded with Cody to let him help with sorting the mama cows from their calves."

Sherry sat forward and angled her a look. "You're different than when I dropped you off at the ranch. You seem happy."

"Things are pretty good." Autumn smiled to herself.

"You're keeping something from me."

Autumn hesitated, but she needed to tell someone. "You know me too well." She leaned forward and lowered her voice. "This is between you and me and no one else."

"I'm your best friend, Autumn. You know you can trust me."

"Cody and I sort of got involved," she admitted. "Nothing we want anyone to know about, though—especially the boys." They already had enough to deal with, without their foster dad's relationship with the housekeeper complicating matters.

Sherry looked worried. "He's your boss, Autumn."

"I know."

"You're not falling for him, are you?"

"I'm not that stupid. I do like him a lot." She also wanted him, so much that she no longer cared that she was setting herself up for future heartache. "But I don't have any fantasies about a life together. It wouldn't work."

"Just make sure you remember that," Sherry said.

"I will, I promise," Autumn replied—and she almost believed herself.

Chapter Seventeen

Autumn was in her apartment Saturday evening, getting ready to take herself out for ice cream and while away the hours until she and Cody could be together, when someone rapped on the door.

Her heart tripped. She and Cody had agreed to meet much later, after the boys went to bed. So why was he knocking at her door at seven-thirty?

She opened it—and found Justin standing there.

"Hi," she said. "Come on in."

The boy stepped inside. "You're dressed up."

In a tank top and denim skirt? Hardly. "I'm going out," she said.

"Oh." The boy hung his head. "Okay. Never mind."

"Tell me what you wanted."

"Tonight we're watching the first two *Star Wars* movies, with popcorn and stuff." He shifted, then lifted one shoulder in a shrug.

"And you want me to join you?" That sounded fun, but it was difficult enough for her and Cody to hide their interest in each other without suffering through the entire evening pretending. "Did you ask your foster brothers if they want me around?"

"They don't care."

"What about Cody?"

"He said sure, but if you don't believe me, ask him yourself. He's in the kitchen."

Autumn followed Justin through the alcove. Cody was measuring popcorn kernels into a cup.

"She wants to talk to you about tonight," the boy told him.

"Justin invited me to your movie night," she said. "What do you think?"

Barely sparing her a glance, Cody pulled the popcorn maker from the cupboard. "It's okay with me."

"Told ya."

"All right, I'll watch movies with you."

"Cool."

"Justin, go ask your foster brothers what kind of pop they want," Cody said.

"Are you sure about this?" Autumn whispered as soon as Justin had left.

"We won't sit together or even glance at each other—though the way you look right now, that won't be easy." Cody's appreciative gaze slid over her, flooding her with familiar heat.

"Stop looking at me like that, or I swear I'll go up in flames. And we both know this isn't the time or the—"

Footsteps announced Justin's return. "Ty wants root beer and—"

Autumn startled, and Cody hastily stepped back. The boy narrowed his eyes. "What's going on in here?"

"We were talking," Cody replied, his expression carefully blank.

Trying hard not to blush, Autumn smiled. "Ty wants root beer. I think I'll have lemonade." She pivoted toward the refrigerator. "What about you, Justin?"

The boy gave her a dirty look and elbowed her aside. "*I'll* get the drinks."

Ignoring the lemonade, he took out four cans of pop.

How much of the conversation had he overheard? Autumn exchanged a nervous glance with Cody.

"Something bothering you, Justin?" Cody asked, reaching for some bowls.

"Nope."

He nodded. "Okay. You and Autumn pass out the napkins and drinks. I'll be in with the popcorn shortly."

HOURS LATER, AFTER the boys had turned in, Cody strolled with Autumn toward the place he'd come to think of as their private piece of heaven—the flat patch of ground under the black elm where they'd spent the past three evenings together.

"I'm worried about Justin. Did you see the dirty look he gave me in the kitchen tonight?" Autumn said as they stopped at the barn for the old quilt. "What if he knows about us?"

Cody grabbed hold of her hand and rubbed his thumb over her knuckles. "He might have sensed something, but you smoothed things out during the movie."

"He did seem fine after I sat beside him and paid him extra attention. But I can't help wondering what he heard."

"Nothing that concerns him. The real issue here is that he wants you to himself. Sorry, kid, but no way."

Cody stopped midstep and tipped up her chin. In the meager light of the new moon, he could barely make out her expression, but he was able to see that her lips had parted—signaling that she expected a kiss. Not about to disappoint her, he tugged her close. With a soft sigh, she twined her arms around his neck and settled against him.

"I've been thinking about this all day," he murmured

when he came up for air. "Come on, let's go to our secret place."

A few minutes later, he spread the quilt over the ground and pulled Autumn down beside him. The usual crickets serenaded them, and somewhere in the distance, a dog barked. He put his arm around her, and she snuggled close.

Contentment filled him. "Would you mind taking the boys shopping for school clothes next week?" he asked.

She pulled away and glanced at him in surprise. "Don't you think they'd rather go with you?"

Cody shook his head. "I've been thinking about this for a few days now. They need an adult female to fuss over them—you see that now with Justin. You like them, and they're all more or less comfortable with you now, so it makes sense that you should take them shopping."

"You're asking me to mother them." She picked up a leaf that had drifted onto the quilt and twirled it. "I don't know whether to be flattered or scared to death."

Wanting her closer, he ran his hand up her smooth, bare arm. "I'm not asking you to be their mom, Autumn. Just do what you always do, and make them feel good about themselves."

She was quiet for a moment, her chin angled thoughtfully. Intrigued by her slightly pursed lips, Cody leaned over and kissed her. When he broke contact some time later, he barely remembered what they'd been talking about.

"What were you saying?" she murmured.

Her ponytail was crooked and she wore that dreamy look that drove him wild. He wanted to kiss her all over again, but first they needed to finish the conversation.

"We were discussing you taking the boys clothes shopping," he reminded her. "Elk Ridge is the closest town with a department store and has plenty of restaurants to choose from for lunch. It'll be a nice excursion. What do you think?"

He wasn't sure why her answer mattered so much, but it did. He sucked in a breath.

"I guess I could take them next Tuesday," she said.

"That's my girl."

He shifted so that her back was to him and she was cradled in the V between his thighs. Propping his chin on the top of her head, he wrapped his arms around her. The sweet scent of lilac and woman wafted in the air.

"I love late-summer nights in Montana," she said. "The air cools down, and the crickets come out.... It's perfect here, just perfect."

"Especially when you have someone to enjoy it with." He sensed that she smiled. "The summer Phil took me in, I used to sleep out here on hot summer nights. It was his way of letting me know he trusted me not to run. I'd lie on my back and count the stars."

"When Heather had company, I used to do the same thing," Autumn said. "I'd imagine all the people in the world looking at the same stars, and wonder what they were thinking. Let's do it now."

Cody moved the quilt from under the tree, and they stretched out, hands behind their heads. Above them, the stars glittered like diamonds.

"Did you ever wish on a star?" he said, his eyes on her instead of the sky.

"All the time, but none of my wishes ever came true."

"What did you wish for?"

"Do you have an hour?" Autumn gave a wry smile.

"I want to know."

"Mostly, I wished for a real family, and a mother who

acted like one instead of a jealous girlfriend. What about you?"

"When I was a naive little kid and didn't know any better, I wished my mom would come back."

After a pensive silence, Autumn said, "If you could have any wish in the world this moment, what would it be?"

"Right now, I'm pretty happy." Happier than he'd been in years. "But if we're talking about the future, my wish would be for the boys to grow up to be healthy, productive men."

"With you there to guide them, they just might."

The conviction in her voice and certainty in her smile made Cody feel as if he'd won a prize. "What do *you* want, Autumn? If you could have anything, what would it be?"

"To go to college." Looking appalled, she clapped her hand to her mouth. "I don't know where that came from. Can you imagine *me* in college?" She let out a nervous laugh.

"What's so funny about that?"

"I could never go. I'm not smart enough."

"I don't get why you think that. You're *really* smart. Who said you weren't?"

"Heather, mostly, and my high school algebra teacher. Plus, if you'd seen my grades…"

Cody wanted to shake them both for putting doubts into her head. He leaned on one elbow and touched her cheek with his knuckle. "Your mom and that teacher are wrong, and you can prove it. Enroll in college and earn a degree."

Autumn moved out of reach and sat up. "I just told you, I don't have the grades—or the money."

Cody sat up, too. "Have you thought about community

college? There's one about an hour's drive from here, and you don't need top grades to get in. It doesn't cost nearly as much as a four-year program, either."

"You really think I could get in?" she asked, eyeing him.

"I *know* it." Wanting to erase her doubtful frown, he expanded on that. "I know you, Autumn, and when you set your mind to do something, it gets done." A few weeks ago he wouldn't have said that, but he knew her better now. "Like not giving up on the boys. You're working miracles with Justin, *and* you're turning into a reasonably decent cook." He gave her a teasing smile about that last part.

Her eyes shone. "No one else has ever said anything so nice to me."

She climbed onto his lap, leaned up and kissed him.

Chapter Eighteen

Cody believed in her. Awed, Autumn held back nothing from her kiss. He'd melted her heart, which felt an awful lot like love. Scared that it might be true—that she was in love him—she almost jerked out of his arms.

But no, she wasn't about to get her heart broken by falling for him. She liked him and that was all, she assured herself. He pulled her against his chest and kissed her with the passion she craved. Her nerves tingled and her body caught fire, and she forgot about everything but how he made her feel.

They exchanged long, deep, popcorn-flavored kisses. Their tongues tangled and their breath mingled. Restless hands, seeking and giving pleasure.

Lost in a haze of desire, she twisted free and straddled him. Groaning, he pushed himself against her, right where she most needed that pressure.

He cupped her breasts, teasing and fondling her until she thought she'd die of pleasure. Wanting to touch him the same way, Autumn slipped her hands under his T-shirt. His back was broad, the muscles taut and the skin hot and smooth.

Cody broke the kiss to pull off his shirt and help Autumn tug her tank top over her head.

Her bra quickly followed. For the first time, she let him see her bare breasts.

He glanced at her and swallowed thickly. "You're even more beautiful than I dreamed."

He wasn't the first man to tell her that, but this time it felt real. Maybe because Cody truly cared. He might not love her, but he felt something.

One finger traced a slow downward path from the upper slope of her breast. He circled her nipple, and she forgot to breathe. He teased the other breast in the same way. When she stirred restlessly, he took her nipple into his mouth.

Autumn lost herself in the sensations—the gentle roughness of his callused palm, the wet swirl of his tongue, the sweet, suckling pull of his lips against her sensitive skin…

Moisture dampened her panties, and tension coiled low in her belly. Needing to be closer to him, she gripped his hips with her thighs. Only her panties and his jeans separated them from joining together.

"Take it easy." Clamping a hand on her hip, Cody held her still and kissed her mouth deeply, his free hand on the inside of her knee. He pushed her skirt up to her waist and slid his palm up her inner thigh. Then he slipped his fingers under the elastic of her panties, and went straight to where she most craved his touch.

A loud moan filled the air. Hers, she realized dimly, before a powerful climax emptied her mind.

When the waves of pleasure eased and she floated back to earth, Cody kissed her fervently.

"I enjoyed that," he said, looking pleased with himself.

Sated and relaxed, she glanced at the erection straining his zipper. "I'm clean, Cody. No diseases. If you want, we can—"

"I'm clean, too. I definitely want to make love with you, Autumn, but when we do, it will be in a bed." He flashed a wicked grin at her. "At least the first time."

Oh, for a bed right here under the stars. "With four teenage boys in the house, we don't exactly have much privacy."

"That's what late nights and locked doors are for. We'll have to be careful and really quiet, though."

Autumn was willing to hold off, but Cody looked as if he needed release now. "We don't have to make love in order for me to give you pleasure," she said.

Heat glittered in his eyes. "I have no doubt of that. But I'd rather wait."

CODY AND AUTUMN made their way back to the house hand in hand. Despite his own sexual frustration, he felt oddly satisfied. Pleasuring her had been almost as good as sex.

A few yards from the house, they stopped to gape at the light blazing through the kitchen and utility room windows.

He frowned. "That's odd. I swear I turned everything off but the light over the kitchen sink."

"You did." Autumn pulled her hand from his. "Do you think one of the boys is awake?"

"Did you see them after the second movie? They were barely able to get up off the couch and drag their butts to bed. They should all be deep in dreamland."

"Well, someone isn't."

"I'll give you two guesses who," Cody said, figuring it must be Justin. He held the utility room door open for Autumn, and then followed her inside.

As he'd suspected, Justin was leaning against the wall waiting for them. He greeted them with a stony expression.

In no mood for a confrontation, Cody kept his tone mild. "It's late. What are you doing up?"

"I wanted to tell Autumn something, but she didn't answer her door. You weren't in your bedroom, either." His eyes narrowed. "Where were you?"

"We took a walk."

Justin cast Autumn a sullen glance, no doubt noting her cockeyed ponytail and kiss-swollen lips. "Yeah, right."

"We were just talking," Autumn said, blushing. "School's starting soon, and Cody asked me to take you and your foster brothers clothes shopping in Elk Ridge. We're going to go next week."

The boy eyed Cody. "Are you coming with us?"

"Hadn't planned on it. Too much to do around here. It'll just be Autumn and you boys."

"What did you want to tell me, Justin?" she asked.

"It's not important."

Cody didn't like the belligerent expression on the boy's face. "What's eating you?"

His narrow shoulders squared and his jaw set, Justin stepped protectively between the two adults, showing Cody a glimpse of the powerful man he would be someday. "I don't like the way you look at Autumn."

What the hell? The past few days, Cody had been extra careful *not* to look at her.

"You shouldn't stare at her like that," Justin said. "Whenever my dad looks at a woman that way, there's always trouble."

So that's what this was about. "I'm not your dad, Justin, and there won't be any trouble here. You have my word."

Autumn touched the boy's forearm. "It's nice that

you're concerned about me, Justin, but I can take care of myself."

The boy gave a reluctant nod, then stepped aside so that he no longer stood between them.

"I want you to know that I trust Cody," she went on. "He's a good man."

The words settled warmly in Cody's chest. He wanted to put his arm around her, but didn't.

"We square now?" he asked the boy.

"Just keep your hands to yourself." Turning on his heel, Justin stalked away.

"He was worried about me," Autumn said. "That's so sweet."

Cody disagreed. "He's overly possessive. I understand that he never had much of a mom and that he's starved for female attention, but he just stepped over the line. What you and I do when we're alone is none of his concern."

"He doesn't seem to agree. What should we do about it?"

Having no idea how to handle the situation, Cody scratched the back of his neck. "First thing Monday morning, I'll get hold of the therapist and have a chat with him."

Autumn nodded, biting her lip. "With Justin up and about late at night, maybe we should cool things off for a bit."

Cody didn't want that. He wanted to make love with Autumn in the very near future. "I'm not letting a kid dictate what I can and can't do," he said.

"I agree, but Justin is so emotionally fragile. He's just beginning to come out of his shell, and I'd hate to do anything to push him back in."

She had a point. Making love would have to wait. Cody gave a grudging nod. "Okay, but I don't like it."

He walked Autumn to the alcove, kissed her lightly on the lips and headed for the stairs.

As SOON AS AUTUMN unlocked her door and stepped into her apartment, she frowned. Once again, something felt off. She couldn't put her finger on what was different, but then she realized what it was.

Someone was in here while I was gone.

Impossible. She'd locked the door and had taken the key with her. All the same, she hurried into her little kitchen. The money can was right where it always was. She unscrewed the cap. The bills appeared undisturbed, but she counted them, anyway. Like before, nothing was missing.

She sagged against the wall in relief. Moments later, she straightened. She still couldn't shake the feeling that someone had been in here. Hugging herself, she walked through the entire apartment, looking for signs of an intruder. As far as she could tell, nothing had been disturbed or taken.

Surely she was imagining things. She was still somewhat dazed from her passionate evening with Cody. Tack on the confrontation with Justin, and she wasn't exactly thinking clearly. That had to be the problem, she assured herself.

Regardless, she intended to tell Cody about this in the morning.

But after a good night's sleep, Autumn changed her mind. If she said something to Cody, he'd question the boys and stir up all kinds of trouble. When she had no proof. What if this was another test of some kind?

She didn't want to fail again, especially when she was getting along so well with everyone.

No, once again, she would keep this to herself.

ALL IN ALL, the shopping trip had been a success, Autumn decided, as she and the boys piled into the Jeep on Tuesday, after a late lunch at an Elk Ridge steak house.

She only wished she wasn't feeling so drained. The past two nights, longing for Cody had kept her tossing and turning. Between that and worrying about Justin...

The therapist had told Cody to give the boy extra attention without going overboard, and it seemed to help. No one had mentioned last Saturday's late-night face-off.

Today Autumn had worked hard to show Justin she cared, while also being attentive to the other boys. Her efforts had paid off. She might be worn-out, but the boys had been in good moods all day.

At the moment, however, they were quiet and still, heavy food and the long day having sapped their energy. Sitting in the passenger seat beside her, Justin cradled his shopping bag as if it contained precious cargo. None of the boys had wanted to store their purchases in the back of the Jeep.

Justin turned on the radio and a hip-hop song filled the car. When the tune ended, Ty spoke. "This is the first time I ever had new clothes."

"One Christmas I got a new sweatshirt and jeans," Eric replied. "But I've never had this many pairs of pants, or shirts."

Autumn smiled at them in the rearview mirror. "You both looked so handsome in those clothes. The girls at your high school will be sure to notice."

Eric blushed, while Ty grinned. "Girls don't care what I wear—they like me all the same."

Noah's laugh was rife with skepticism. "You're so full of it. Justin and I got cool stuff, too."

"You did," Autumn said. "You'll fit right in with the other kids at school."

"What about getting our hair cut?" Eric said.

"You'll have to talk to Cody about that, but there's a great stylist in Saddlers Prairie. Her name is Anita. Maybe he'll take you to her salon after your physicals." Autumn made a mental note to speak to Cody about that.

Another song started. Justin cranked up the radio and the rest of the way home, no one uttered a word.

Autumn's thoughts homed in on Cody and the last time they'd been together on the blanket under the stars. No man had ever made her feel so hungry and restless.

Even better, he believed she was smart enough to go to college.

As badly as she ached to be with him, she told herself that the decision to pull back was a good one, and not just because of Justin. For her own sake. To keep her heart safe.

Yet every time Cody brushed against her, every time his eyes fixed on her in a private, stolen look, the desire that always simmered inside her flared so hot that she couldn't think of anything but being alone with him.

As soon as the opportunity presented itself, she knew they would make love. The question was, when? Cody wanted the first time to be in a bed, but she didn't care.

"Autumn, how come you aren't listening?" Justin said over the sound of the radio.

"To the song?"

"No, to me."

"Sorry," she said, turning off the music. "What did you say?"

"When we get back, do we have to do chores?"

"Remember what Cody said this morning?"

"That me and Eric need to weed and water the garden when we get back," Ty replied.

Noah leaned forward. "Justin and I are supposed to

muck out the horses' stalls. Then we all get to swim in the river."

"Except Justin." Autumn glanced at the boy. "It'll be a couple more days for you. You can go out to the swing, though."

The boy's snort let her know what he thought of that idea. He'd tried it once, at her insistence, but hadn't experienced the same sense of exhilaration she had.

"What are you making for dinner tonight, Autumn?" Eric asked.

Over the past few weeks, her cooking had improved by leaps and bounds. She wasn't the best cook around, but Cody and the boys no longer complained. "I thought I'd bake a chicken—if Justin will help with the recipe. He's such a good cook."

He smiled proudly.

The rest of the boys licked their lips, and she barely suppressed a laugh. And to think she'd once been scared of recipes.

She'd been at Hope Ranch nearly a month, and each day she enjoyed her job more. The time seemed to fly by, and she half wished it would slow down. When her sixty days ended, she was going to miss working there. Miss the boys, and most of all, Cody.

"You look sad," Justin said.

"I'm fine. We're almost home."

Home. The word just slipped out. It wasn't her home and never would be.

Filled with melancholy, Autumn pasted a bright smile on her face and turned into the driveway.

Chapter Nineteen

The Saturday evening before Labor Day, the boys voted to skip watching a movie and play video games instead. Sprawled in an armchair in the great room, Cody fiddled with his iPad, while Ty, Noah and Eric sat huddled together on the sofa. Instead of joining his foster brothers, Justin, who usually begged to play, had wandered into the kitchen to see Autumn.

Despite the extra attention Cody and Autumn gave the boy and the fact that his hand was finally healed, Justin spent most of his spare time hovering around Autumn like a lovesick puppy. It wasn't healthy, and it was getting old.

"I'll be back," Cody told the boys.

After a day spent canning garden produce at Joan's, Autumn had brought back several dozen jars of bread-and-butter pickles, tomatoes and green beans. Cody found her in the pantry with Justin, putting the goods on the shelves.

"What are you two up to?" Cody said, leaning against the pantry doorjamb.

"Hi." Autumn smiled softly, and his heart thumped hard in his chest. "Justin's helping me organize this stuff. We're also planning the menu for next week, so I'll know what to pick up at Spenser's."

"On a Saturday night? The other boys are playing video games," he told Justin. "Don't you want to join them?"

"I'd rather hang out with Autumn."

"She's supposed to be off on weekends. She already spent her Saturday canning food for us. She deserves a break," Cody said, locking his gaze with hers. Silently letting her see that he wanted her.

Her pupils dilated, leaving no doubt that she desired him, too. Not being together was killing him.

"Autumn?" Justin said, frowning. "Do you want me to go?"

She tore her gaze from Cody. "Go where?"

The boy's mouth flattened. "When Cody's around, you don't even know I'm here."

Autumn blushed. "That's not true."

"Save it for someone who cares," he said, storming out of the pantry.

"What just happened?" Autumn asked.

"Like I've been saying, he doesn't want to share you," Cody replied in a low voice. "I just checked the community college schedule. Classes start at the end of September, and registration is open now." He handed over the iPad. "Here, have a look at the programs they offer. You can register online."

"I don't know, Cody." She fiddled with her ponytail, the movement thrusting her breasts forward.

Breasts he knew the feel and taste of. He swallowed. "Won't hurt to look at the website. And hey, if the boys see you going to college, maybe they'll start thinking about going themselves someday."

"You forget I'm leaving in early October." She brushed past him into the kitchen, her lilac scent wrapping around him.

His body tightened painfully. "We haven't had any interest in the housekeeper job," he said, his voice rough. "You could apply."

She seemed surprised. "But the Burger Palace is looking for a new manager. With my restaurant background, I think I'm qualified."

"You'd be bored in ten minutes." He tipped up her chin. "At least think about staying on here."

Yearning and need colored her face. "When you look at me like that, I can't think."

He lowered his gaze to her mouth, and the urge to kiss her gripped him. "I need to be with you outside," he said.

Her eyes darkened in understanding. "We can't. What about the boys?"

"It's a nice night," he called out, loudly enough that they could hear. "Anyone care to come check on the stars with Autumn and me?"

"In the middle of a video game, when I'm winning?" Ty hooted.

"Don't stay out too long," Eric exclaimed, "or Justin'll get jealous."

"No, I won't!"

"We'll be back shortly." Cody grabbed Autumn's hand and tugged her through the utility room and out the door.

The past few nights the weather had turned, and she shivered in the cool night air.

"Come here and let me warm you up." He pulled her into the shadows and kissed her. Hard, with all the hunger he felt.

She molded herself to his body, and he backed her up against the house. With his hands on her breasts, he kissed her again.

Moaning, she wrapped her calf around his legs and caught his lower lip between her teeth.

Blood pounded in his head. He thrust his hips against her. "I want to be inside you, Autumn."

"I know," she said, sounding as if she'd been running. "Sometimes I think I'll burn up from all the wanting."

He rested his forehead against hers. "School starts Tuesday. As soon as the bus picks up Ty and Eric, and I get back from dropping Justin and Noah at their school, I'm going to make love with you."

Her searing kiss all but wiped out his thoughts.

Some time later, his erection still pulsing, Cody straightened Autumn's top and they headed silently back to the house.

WARMED BY CODY'S dizzying kisses and the promise of making love with him just three days from now, Autumn brought his iPad into her apartment. She sat down on the sofa and looked up the community college website. The school offered all kinds of courses, even some in psychology. She enjoyed helping the boys. Maybe with a degree in psychology, she could get a job helping others.

Excitement churned in her. Could she really do this?

It didn't take long for doubt to set in. Regardless of whether Cody believed in her, she wasn't college material. He was right about the Burger Palace, though. She'd hate working there.

She typed in Craigslist and searched for local job openings. An ad that was surely Cody's caught her eye.

Ranch housekeeper wanted for foster dad and four teenage boys in Saddlers Prairie, Montana. Good wages, apartment and board provided. Available October.

He'd suggested that she should apply for the job, and she wanted to. But as things stood, she was barely hold-

ing on to her heart. The longer she stayed, the greater
the risk was that she'd fall in love with Cody. She knew
how that would end—in heartache and pain.

And making love won't lead to heartache?

Autumn wanted him too much to back down from the
chance to be with him. She was strong enough to protect
her heart until she left the ranch, she assured herself.

Wasn't she?

"ENJOY YOUR FIRST day of school," Autumn said, smiling
as Ty and Eric headed out Tuesday morning. Their bus
would pick them up at the end of the driveway. "Anita
gave you great haircuts. You both look so handsome."

Grumbles filled the air, but underneath, the two boys
were all nervous energy and excitement. Autumn said a
silent prayer that they'd like their new teachers and make
some friends.

Minutes later, she pulled her sweater close and walked
Noah and Justin to Cody's truck. As the boys were climbing into the cab, Cody leaned over and spoke in a low
voice, his eyes filled with promise. "I'll see you in under
thirty minutes."

Her nerves thrummed. "Your bedroom or mine?"

"Mine."

Once the truck had rumbled down the driveway, Autumn headed inside. She hadn't eaten yet and made herself a piece of toast. She managed to get a few bites down.
By the time she brushed her teeth, he'd been gone nearly
twenty minutes. After her shower this morning, she'd
misted herself with the lilac scent she knew he liked. If
only she owned a slinky teddy to change into. Unfortunately, she'd dumped all her naughty lingerie at the thrift
store in Bozeman.

Cody would just have to take her as she was. Autumn

traded her blouse, jeans and underwear for a robe, and climbed the stairs. Cody had left the bedroom drapes shut, but the morning sun streamed through the skylight, straight onto the bed. The blanket was neatly turned back in invitation.

Should she slip out of her robe and climb into bed, or sit down in an armchair and wait for him? In the end, she decided to go meet him in the kitchen.

She was halfway down the stairs when she heard the truck pull in. He was back.

UNABLE TO WAIT another minute to see Autumn, Cody toed out off his boots, yanked off his socks and strode quickly toward the stairs. She was waiting for him on the steps, her hair lovely and loose around her shoulders. She wore a knee-length robe, belted at the waist. The deep V neckline revealed her generous cleavage.

"Aut—" His voice cracked, and he had to clear his throat. "Autumn."

"Hi." She gave a nervous smile, untied her robe and let it fall at her feet.

She was completely naked. Cody swallowed. Her body was perfect. *She* was perfect—and his.

With his eyes locked on her, he pulled his T-shirt over his head, unbuttoned and unzipped his jeans and stepped out of them and his boxers. She glanced at his erection and her eyes widened.

He headed toward her, stopping on the riser below her, so that their eyes were on the same level. His body urged him to pull her close and take her right there on the steps, but she deserved better.

"I like your hair down," he said, his voice oddly hoarse.

With hands that trembled, he tucked it behind her ears

and cupped her face. Instead of kissing her, he traced the smooth column of her neck and the delicate lines of her collarbone with his fingertips. Then he slid his hand lower, to the rise of her breasts.

Before he even reached the pink areolae, her nipples tightened. He slowly moved toward their beaded tips, enjoying her sharp intake of breath. His intention was to continue exploring the rest of her body, but those aroused points distracted him.

He leaned in, the scent of lilacs and woman filling his senses. He flicked his tongue over her nipples.

Autumn moaned softly. "Cody, I need to sit down."

So did he. Lifting her so that she gripped his hips, and kissing her deeply, he started up the stairs. With each step, her soft, naked bottom pressed against his erection. Killing him.

Somehow he made it to the landing. On the way to the bed, she raked her fingers over his back, while kissing his face and his chest. Making him so hot, he was afraid he'd embarrass himself.

"Easy," he growled.

"I don't want easy."

Desire roared in him. Consumed by need, he laid her on the bed, trapped her arms over her head and kissed his way down her smooth stomach and then lower.

Releasing her wrists, he moved his hand between her legs and slid two fingers inside.

She made that sweet sound of desire again and moved against him.

Leaving his fingers inside her, he touched her most sensitive place with his tongue. A tremor ran through her, echoing in his own body. He tongued her again, until she cried out and climaxed.

Cody wanted the same release—while he was buried

deep inside her. He jerked the bedside table drawer open and reached for a foil packet.

"Let me." Autumn took her damn time rolling the thing over his shaft.

About to lose control, he pushed her away. "I'll do it."

As soon as he'd sheathed himself, he covered her with his body and entered her in one thrust.

Home.

Autumn moaned. "Do that again, harder."

He thrust again, deeper, faster, his world condensed into the place where he was joined with her.

Tightening around him, she answered with her own sounds of pleasure.

They shattered at the same time.

When the earth righted itself he rolled beside her, and she nestled her head on his chest. Sunshine streaming through the skylight lit her beautiful body, all flushed with desire.

A profound sense of peace filled him, a tranquillity he hadn't felt in a long time—maybe never. He kissed the top of her head. "That was definitely worth waiting for."

"The best sex I've ever had. You're a wonderful lover and a wonderful man, Cody Naylor."

His chest swelled with emotion. He curled his hand over her hip. Autumn shifted, her silky hair teasing his skin. Already, he wanted her again.

He stared up at the flawless blue sky, trying to gauge whether he had time to make love with her again. Imagined what it would be like to spend every night with her and wake up beside her every morning.

Slow down. He wasn't ready for that, and he was pretty sure Autumn wasn't, either. They'd never discussed the future. He was confusing great sex with deeper feelings, that was all. Nothing had changed from before. The trouble was, he wasn't sure what it had been before.

Suddenly, he needed space.

He tensed, and Autumn shifted away from him. "You need to get to work, and so do I."

Grateful that she understood, he sat up. "I'll get your robe."

COVERING HERSELF WITH the blanket, Autumn watched as Cody padded naked from the bedroom. Her heart was so full it overflowed, spilling liquid sunshine through her entire body. Which wasn't a good thing.

Sometime during their lovemaking, she'd forgotten to protect her heart, had released it and given it to him. Now she felt vulnerable and a little scared.

Cody didn't love her, she was sure. And that was okay. She just needed time alone, to pull herself together.

He returned to the room and handed her the robe. Leaned down and kissed her softly.

Steeling herself against a wash of tender feelings, she forced a smile. "I wasn't sure what you wanted to do for lunch today, so I packed a sack lunch. It's in the fridge."

"Great. School lets out at three. I'll pick up Noah and Justin and drop them off, but don't expect me back at the house until dinner."

Grateful for the hours of solitude ahead, Autumn nodded. "See you then."

Chapter Twenty

After showering away all the signs of Cody's lovemaking, and getting dressed, Autumn felt more in control. She pulled half a dozen chicken breasts from the basement freezer, made chocolate chip cookies and did the laundry. It was a warm day, and she opened the windows in the kitchen.

She was heating up that morning's coffee and wondering what to do next when Sherry called.

"You'll never guess what—Shawn proposed! Wait, hold on a sec." She clicked off to answer the phone in the receiving department of the feed store where she worked.

Autumn wished she could share in her friend's excitement, but wasn't exactly in the mood to listen to Sherry's chatter. Still, she wasn't about to put a damper on the moment. While she waited for Sherry to come back on the phone, she fixed her coffee and carried it to the table.

"I'm back," Sherry said.

"Congratulations! Tell me everything."

"Okay, but if the phone rings I'll have to put you on hold again."

Sherry described how Shawn had proposed the day before, during a late-afternoon Labor Day picnic. They'd both asked for the day off on Thursday and Friday to drive to Billings and go ring shopping. Sherry bubbled on about their wedding, planned for early November.

Pleased for her friend, Autumn made the appropriate comments.

"The boys started school today, right?" Sherry said. "I thought you'd be happy, but you sound the opposite."

Autumn wasn't about to pretend. She told her friend what had happened with Cody, and that she loved him. "You warned me to be careful," she finished. "I should've listened."

"You never know. Cody could be in love with you, too."

"He likes me and the sex was amazing, but you and I both know there's no future for us."

"Have you ever discussed it?"

"Does his asking me to apply to be his permanent housekeeper count?"

"No wonder you're blue. What are you going to do?"

Autumn sighed. "Look for work while I finish my time here, then move on."

"I mean, what are you going to do about Cody? You live under the same roof, and you can't exactly avoid him."

"No, but I'm pretty good at hiding my feelings."

"With your expressive face? Ha."

Autumn sighed. "I don't have a choice, Sherry. Cody can't know that I love him." Otherwise she'd never survive the next three weeks.

"Good luck. Oops, here comes the foreman. Call me if you need to talk."

Autumn finished her coffee. The house was too quiet, and she needed something to do. Tuesday wasn't her usual cleaning day, but she cleaned anyway, washing windows and scrubbing the porch cushions.

By midafternoon she was sick of her own company and eager for the boys to come home. Ty and Eric arrived first, bursting through the utility room and into the kitchen.

As usual, they were famished, and they quickly devoured the cheese and crackers Autumn had set out, followed by chocolate chip cookies and several glasses of milk.

Autumn sat with them while they ate. "Tell me about your school."

"I've never been in a school without graffiti," Ty said. "Even the bathrooms are clean."

"I had a burrito for lunch," Eric said. "And pie. It was good."

Ty mentioned several of the girls in his classes, and he and Eric compared teachers. They sounded like normal kids.

When they finished their snack, they retreated to their room to change into their work clothes.

Not long after the boys headed outside to do their chores, Autumn heard the purr of Cody's truck. Her heart stuttered in her chest, and she thanked her lucky stars that he wasn't coming inside. She wasn't ready to face him just yet.

Noah and Justin flew in the door, dropped their backpacks and toed off their shoes. Like the older boys, they were starving. Autumn served them the same snack and, as she had with the older boys, joined them at the table. "How was your day?"

"Mrs. Dawson is nice," Noah said.

Justin curled his lip. "Our school is really small. One room—that's wack."

Autumn barely registered his words. Was that Cody's voice outside? Maybe he hadn't rejoined his crew after dropping off the boys. Maybe he was about to walk through the door.

Justin looked at her strangely. "Did you hear what I said about school?"

"That it's wack," she repeated, nervously lacing her fingers together.

The boy frowned at her as if she was crazy. "What's wrong with you?"

"I was—I thought I heard Cody outside."

"So?"

Not about to show the turmoil inside her, Autumn drew in a calming breath and tried to pull herself together. "Nothing. Go on."

"Never mind. When do you want to start the chicken?"

She stared blankly at Justin.

"We're having stir-fry chicken tonight, remember? You said I could help make it."

"That's right, I did. We'll start as soon as you change clothes and finish your chores."

THANKS TO A BULL breaking though a fence and injuring his leg, Cody didn't make it home until after six. When he entered the kitchen, Autumn and the boys were filling their glasses and carrying platters of food to the table.

"Sorry I'm late," he said.

"No problem. We haven't started eating yet."

Autumn's smile seemed forced, and he knew he should've let Doug and some of the other men handle the bull, and come home earlier. The truth was, he'd stayed away because he wasn't sure what to say to her. *I really liked the sex, but I'm not sure what I'm doing and need space* wouldn't fly.

Dinner was decent enough, and the boys were full of

stories about their new schools. Autumn smiled and con-
versed with them, but she barely glanced Cody's way.

Yep, he'd screwed up. He set down his fork. "How was
your day, Autumn?"

"Not bad." Her cheeks flushed, and uncertainty flashed
in her eyes before she turned the lazy Susan and reached
for the pitcher of iced tea.

Was she also having second thoughts about this morning? He knew she'd enjoyed the sex as much as he had,
but they really needed to talk.

"Autumn!" Justin said in a loud, frustrated voice. "I
asked you if you'd help me with my vocabulary words."

She gave a start. "I'd be happy to."

Ty eyed Cody. "Aren't you gonna remind Justin to
watch his tone?" Before Cody could form a reply, the boy
snorted. "Guess you're not listening, either."

"I was thinking about tonight," Cody said. "No TV
until you finish your homework."

Eric gaped at him as if he'd grown an extra nose.
"We just went over that. What's the deal with you and
Autumn?"

"Nothing," they answered at the same time.

"Bull," Noah countered.

The rest of the meal passed in strained silence.

While the boys cleared the table, Cody beckoned Autumn into the hall. "Are you okay about this morning?"
he whispered.

"Absolutely. It was wonderful."

Her smile reassured him, and he let out a breath. "The
best."

His body stirred. He was starting to reconsider his
need for space when she turned away from him.

"I should put the leftovers in the fridge."

Okay, then. Maybe she needed some distance, too.

Once the kitchen was clean, everyone gathered in the great room. Sitting with a laptop at a small table in one corner, Autumn helped Justin look up his vocabulary words. On the other side of the room, Cody coached Eric in basic algebra, while Ty read a chapter in his history book and Noah worked on his "What I Did This Summer" paper.

Suddenly, Justin snapped the laptop shut. "Never mind, Autumn, I'll do it myself."

She nodded and stood. "I'm going to bed. Good night, everyone."

Cody glanced at the clock. It was only eight-thirty.

The boys exchanged glances.

As soon as she left the room, Justin narrowed his eyes at Cody. "What'd you do to her?"

Cody had no idea, but he was pretty sure she'd lied to him earlier. She wasn't okay about this morning.

While the boys finished their homework, Cody knocked on Autumn's door. She didn't answer. Maybe she really was tired and was already asleep.

But when he turned in two hours later, he was still scratching his head, wondering how to fix whatever was wrong.

In the morning rush of getting the boys fed and out the door there was no time for Cody to pull Autumn aside. When he returned home after dropping off Justin and Noah at school, she was out. He resolved to talk to her that afternoon, no matter what.

He came in the house with Noah and Justin after driving them home. Autumn looked surprised, especially when he sat down at the table with them. As the boys crammed their mouths with thick slices of bread and butter, Cody attempted to make small talk and did a pretty lousy job of it. The boys quickly finished their snack and left the table.

Autumn jumped up to clear the mess.

"Sit back down. Please," Cody said. Wide-eyed, she did as he asked. Aware that the boys could walk in at any time, he cleared his throat. "We need to talk about yesterday."

"We already did." She traced a ring on the table left by a milk glass. "Everything's fine."

"It doesn't *feel* fine. You're tense, I'm tense and it makes the boys tense."

She bit her lip, her eyes sad and confused. "I've decided to apply for the manager job at the Burger Palace."

Disappointment bit him, sharp and stinging. "You're not staying here, then."

"Cody, I—"

"Autumn, I need help with my homework," Justin said, returning to the kitchen.

"Not right now," she replied, her eyes locked with Cody's.

"You don't want to help me?"

Cody tore his gaze from her to frown at the boy. "We're trying to have a conversation here," he said, wishing he'd invited her outside to talk. "Go on out and water the garden."

"Noah's supposed to water today, but he's in the bathroom. I'm supposed to pick."

"Then switch. Now go."

"Yes, *sir.*" Justin shot Autumn an accusing look before stalking off.

The utility door slammed hard.

"What the hell?" Cody muttered.

"Did you see his face? He's hurt."

"Because you wanted to finish a conversation with me? He'll get over it."

Autumn stood. "All the same, I think I'd better go talk to him."

SHADING HER EYES against the afternoon sun, Autumn approached Justin. "You're upset," she said softly. "I wish you weren't."

He didn't react, and she wasn't sure he'd even heard her over the loud hiss of the hose.

Suddenly, he spun toward her. "When he's around, you don't even notice me!"

This wasn't the first time he'd accused her of paying Cody too much attention, and in a way he was right. When Cody was near, he was all she could think about. That didn't mean she didn't care about Justin or his foster brothers.

"It's true that I've been a little distracted lately, but I definitely notice you, Justin. You're a great kid and I care about you a lot." She touched his shoulder.

His face dark with anger, he stiffened. "Don't touch me—ever!"

Frightened, Autumn raised her hand and backed away.

His reaction shocked her. Over the past few weeks, she'd put her hand on his shoulder countless times and given him numerous hugs and he'd seemed to appreciate her gestures of affection. "I'd like to straighten this out," she said, her voice shaking. "Please, can we talk about it?"

"Just go away."

His lips thinned before he ducked his head, and Autumn knew that for now, any conversation was out. "Okay, if that's what you want," she said. "If you change your mind, I'll be inside."

The cool breeze carried a hint of fall. Rubbing her arms, she returned to the house.

When she reached the kitchen, the table was clean and Cody was drying his hands on a towel.

Grateful that he was still here, Autumn explained what had happened. "He's angry, Cody, more so than I've even seen him. I feel terrible."

"It's not your fault."

He started to reach for her, and changed his mind, grabbing hold of her hand instead. Hanging on tight, Autumn absorbed his comforting grasp. For one long moment, everything seemed right with the world. Then he pulled away. Missing his reassuring warmth, she clasped her hands together at her waist.

"Too bad this is only Wednesday," he said, "because Justin needs that Saturday therapy session *now*. I'll contact his therapist again."

When he's around, you don't even notice me. Autumn sighed. "I feel like I let him down, like I failed one of his tests."

"You haven't. You're still here for him—at least for now." Cody scrubbed his hand over his face and blew out a breath. "I'd better call the therapist now, before he leaves for the day."

"I'll start dinner."

As upset as Autumn was about Justin, she felt better about Cody. The tension between them had faded. He would never love her, but they both cared about Justin and his foster brothers.

While she cooked sloppy joes for dinner, she thought about the boys. Ty, Eric and Noah seemed to be adjusting well to school and ranch life. Justin had made progress, too—until recently. Autumn felt responsible for his latest problems. She also felt guilty about leaving all of them in a few weeks.

She needed to make things right with Justin. She just needed to figure out how.

Chapter Twenty-One

Wednesday night, Cody lay in bed tossing and turning, his mind in turmoil. Despite the reassurance from Justin's therapist, he was uneasy about the boy. For every step forward, Justin seemed to take two steps back, and Cody felt helpless.

Autumn appeared to hold the key to the boy's well-being. She belonged at the ranch with Cody and the kids, not at some dead-end job.

He wasn't about to let her walk out of his life or theirs. Once she moved out, he intended to ask her on a date, and make sure she visited often.

Cody turned onto his side. He couldn't seem to get comfortable, especially with the sheet twisted around his legs. Jerking it from the bed, he shook it out and smelled Autumn's lilac perfume.

Desire burned inside him. His chest brimmed with emotion, and he wished to God she was lying there with him. Not just for the sex, but so that they could talk privately and without interruption about Justin and anything else under the sun.

Aching for her, Cody finally fell asleep.

"HAVE A GOOD day at school, and see you this afternoon," Autumn said as Cody ushered Noah and Justin out the door on Thursday morning.

Still angry, Justin cold-shouldered her. Leery of his hostility, even Noah veered away from him.

Autumn stared after them, filled with apprehension and having no idea what to do to help.

"Two more days before he sees his therapist," Cody murmured. "Hang in there."

"You, too."

She let out a heavy sigh and sat down at the table with her toast and the Burger Palace job application. This was a good time to fill it out and drop it off. Autumn couldn't get excited about it, though. She didn't really want to work at a fast-food place.

The truth was, she didn't want to leave the ranch. But she was in love with Cody, and she had no choice but to go.

She was sitting glumly, tapping the application with a pen and wishing Sherry hadn't gone to Billings with Shawn, when the phone rang.

"It's Joan. I happen to have this morning off. Do you have time for a cup of coffee?"

The mere sound of the woman's voice cheered Autumn up. After spending the previous Saturday together, learning how to can vegetables, she felt closer to her new friend. Close enough to confide in her. "As a matter of fact, I could use your advice. I'll be right over."

In no time, she was sitting at her friend's kitchen table, sipping coffee.

"You mentioned needing advice?" Joan asked. She looked unusually happy today, as if she was about to burst with excitement.

"I want you to explain the big smile on your face first," Autumn said.

"You can't tell anyone because I haven't even told Doug."

"I won't, I promise. Everything we say this morning is between us, agreed?"

"Agreed." Joan beckoned her closer. "I'm ten days late. Just before I called you, I took a pregnancy test."

"And?"

Joan nodded, and Autumn laughed. She rose and hugged her. "I'm so happy for you."

Also envious. To her embarrassment, her eyes filled with tears.

Joan's smile faded. "What's wrong?"

Autumn swiped at her eyes. "I don't want to put a damper on your joy. I really am thrilled."

"I know you are. Now tell me what's bothering you."

"I made a huge mistake," she confessed. "I've fallen in love with Cody."

"I don't blame you. He's a great guy." Joan frowned. "Don't tell me he isn't interested in you. Is he crazy?"

Autumn couldn't help but smile at her friend's indignation. "He likes me well enough, but he's not in love with me."

She let the rest of the story tumble out, explaining that she wanted to stay at the ranch and why she couldn't. "With time and distance, I'll be okay," she said.

She also shared her fears about Justin. "He was doing really well. But when Cody and I started to like each other…"

"He's just jealous," Joan said.

"It goes beyond that. He doesn't think I even see him anymore. That's how I felt when I was his age, and it's the worst feeling in the world. I don't know what to do."

"He's a troubled boy. He needs help. What about his therapist?"

"Cody spoke with him yesterday. He believes we're doing everything right. But don't you get it, Joan? I made things worse." Autumn bit her lip. "I let him down, and I don't know how to make it up to him."

"Let me get this straight. By falling in love with Cody you let Justin down." When Autumn nodded, Joan shook her head. "That doesn't make any sense. He's what, fourteen? Teenagers always overdramatize things—or so my friends with kids that age tell me. He'll come around eventually."

THAT AFTERNOON, AUTUMN was pulling out a recipe for tea biscuits—Justin loved them—when she realized she was out of baking powder, which showed how distracted she'd been lately. She could've stopped at Spenser's after visiting with Joan. Instead, she had to make a special trip now.

She glanced at the application that had sat on the table all day. If she'd bothered to complete it, she could drop it off on the way. But she hadn't. Tonight, she promised, moving it to the café table in her apartment.

Knowing the boys would be home soon, she set out snacks, propped a note on the toaster explaining where she was, and headed out.

When she returned home an hour later, Ty and Eric were in the yard, working on the garden. Autumn waved. She saw Noah walking toward a pasture near the barn where the horses grazed. There was no sign of Justin, but his backpack was on a kitchen chair.

After setting the groceries on the counter, Autumn headed for the apartment to drop off her purse. She started to unlock her door and then realized it was already unlocked.

Frowning, she pushed it open. Justin was in her kitchen, stuffing money from her can into his pockets.

"What are you doing?" she asked, shock making her voice shrill.

He froze, his eyes wide and scared. Then his face closed. "What does it look like? I'm stealing your money. Then I'm running away from this dump."

"Why, Justin?"

"Because you're leaving!" He picked up the job application, crumpled it into a ball and lobbed it at her. "You're just like my mom! You don't want me in your life."

The boy's leap in logic was completely off base. Wanting him to understand, Autumn tried to explain. "That isn't about you, Justin. It's…" Not about to share her reasons with him, she started again. "Could we please sit down and talk?"

Justin crossed his arms. "Why should I *ever* talk to you?"

"Because I care about you too much to let you run away and be sentenced to juvenile detention over a misunderstanding. I don't think you want that, either."

The boy's bottom lip trembled. He blinked hard against a sheen of tears.

Autumn's eyes filled, too. She pulled out both chairs and sat down at the table. "Talk to me. Please."

Sniffling, Justin pulled her money from his pockets and stuffed the bills back into the can. He replaced the lid, and pushed the container toward Autumn. Then, like a neglected vegetable plant, he wilted onto the chair.

"You've been in my apartment before, haven't you?" she asked softly.

He nodded miserably. "I picked the lock." He swallowed thickly. "I never took anything the other times, though." He studied her through pain-drenched eyes. "Why are you leaving us?"

"You've always known I'd only be here for sixty days."

"I know, but I thought… I want you to stay."

If he only knew how much she wanted that, too. She

glanced at the balled-up job application on the floor. "You probably noticed that I haven't filled out the form yet. I was just looking at it."

"You're still leaving."

"That doesn't mean we can't always be friends."

He hung his head forlornly, and Autumn's heart broke. "I don't know about you, but I really need a hug," she said.

Keeping his head down, he shrugged one shoulder. Autumn pushed her chair closer and put her arms around him.

His thin body shook with noisy sobs. "I'm sorry."

"I know, sweetie." They both needed a tissue. "Let me grab some Kleenex."

She handed him the box and dabbed her own eyes. "Feel better?" she asked.

"Not really," Justin said, but he sat up straighter.

"What you did was wrong, Justin, but I forgive you. I think you should tell Cody."

Fear crossed his face. "You said you don't want me to go to juvie."

"I don't, but Cody needs to know what you did."

"Can't you tell him?"

"He needs to hear it from you. If you want, I'll stand beside you."

After a few tense moments, the boy nodded.

"I'll try to reach Cody on his cell now," Autumn said. "It will probably take him a while to get home. You stay here and wait."

CODY WAS IN the south pasture, about to mount Diablo and head home, when Autumn called. "It's Justin," she said, sounding both breathless and weary. "Something's happened."

Cody's stomach turned over. "Did he cut himself again? Are you okay? Is he?"

"We're both fine, but you need to come home right away."

"I'll be there in ten minutes."

Troubled despite Autumn's reassurance that she and Justin were all right, Cody urged Diablo into a gallop.

Long before he reached the house, he saw her in the distance, waiting for him by the barn. His chest expanded at the sight of her, and like a swift kick in the rear, he suddenly understood.

He was in love with Autumn.

His heart thudded as hard as Diablo's hooves against the packed earth. She was everything he'd ever wanted—smart, beautiful, passionate and great with the boys. The perfect woman.

He wanted to whoop for joy.

But was she even interested in a long-term relationship with him? Cody didn't know, but he intended to find out.

As Diablo closed the distance to the barn and Cody saw her face, his elation dimmed. Her eyes were huge and worried, her ponytail was cockeyed and her teeth clenched her bottom lip.

He dismounted and slapped Diablo's flank. The horse trotted into the barn. He saw Ty, Eric and Noah standing nearby, but he hurried past them to where Autumn stood. He clasped her by the shoulders and peered into her eyes. "Where's Justin? What happened?"

She glanced at the gaping boys. "Let's talk in the barn."

Inside, she sank onto a bale of hay.

Nickering, Diablo wandered over. Cody removed the horse's saddle and led him to his stall. His horse needed to be brushed, fed and watered, but that could wait. Raising his eyebrows in question, Cody leaned against the rough wood wall planking.

"Before I explain, I want you to know that this is my fault," Autumn said. "Please remember that."

Growing more concerned by the moment, Cody frowned. "Just spit it out."

"I went out this afternoon. When I came back, I caught Justin in my apartment. He was stealing from my money can and about to run away, but I talked him out of it."

Cody's jaw dropped. "He *what*?"

"He was upset and acting out because I get so distracted. I didn't know I'd end up caring this much about you—" Her voice broke and she paused to wipe her eyes.

Even sniffling, she was beautiful. Filled with love, he pushed away from the wall. Kneeling at her feet, he took her hands in his.

"Autumn, are you saying you love me?"

She nodded. "I'm afraid so. I've been trying to hide my feelings, but I can't anymore."

"That's good, because I love you, too."

She looked so surprised that he laughed.

"I've never met a woman like you. You're stubborn and you get mad at me a lot, but your heart is as big as this ranch. Don't ever change." He kissed her, holding nothing back. "Now, let's go talk to Justin."

HALF AN HOUR later, everything was settled. Justin had apologized and agreed to make it up to Autumn by taking out the trash every day, cleaning all the bathrooms for a month and promising to speak up when something bothered him.

Cody's stomach growled, but dinner would have to wait. "Brush down Diablo and feed and water him for me, will you, Justin? He's in his stall. Also, let everyone know we're having a group meeting in fifteen minutes."

Justin looked wary. "Are you going to tell the guys what I did?"

"That's not my story to tell. This is about something else."

The boy let out a relieved breath, nodded and left, shutting the apartment door behind him.

"I'm glad that's over. Come here." Cody pulled Autumn onto the sofa and sat beside her. He kissed her, and then kissed her again.

With a soft sigh, she snuggled closer. "Why did you call a group meeting?"

"Because I want the boys to know how much I love you."

Her eyes widened.

"Unless you think I shouldn't."

"You should. I'm so happy."

He laced his fingers with hers, stood, and pulled them both up. "Come on, let's go."

In the great room, everyone took the same places as on the first day Autumn had arrived. Since then, so much had changed, in ways she'd never imagined. Cody stood behind her, his hand on her shoulder.

"What's the deal?" Ty asked.

Noah squinted at Justin. "You look like you've been crying."

"Whoa, dude," Eric said.

Justin flushed. "I was going to run away this afternoon, but I changed my mind. I want to live here with all of you."

Ty sat back and nodded. "Cool."

"Since Justin's being so honest, I will be, too," Autumn said. "I almost applied for a job at the Burger Palace, but I can't leave you." She smiled up at Cody. "*Any* of you. So you can remove the ad for a new housekeeper from Craigslist."

Cody squeezed her shoulder. "The ad stays, but I'd like you to keep the job until I find a replacement."

She looked puzzled. "But you asked me to stay. I thought you liked the way I keep house."

"I do, but when we get married, you'll need someone to help with all the work."

"Is that a proposal?"

Before answering, Cody glanced at the boys. They all grinned and nodded. "If you'll have me—us," he said.

Autumn beamed. "I will, and I do."

Epilogue

Seated in the high school auditorium with a hundred other excited families, as proud as if Ty were her birth son, Autumn leaned across Cody and whispered to Eric, Noah and Justin. "Ty's next."

Cody aimed his cell phone at the stage, and the boys sat forward.

"Tyler Johnson," the portly high school principal said.

Beaming, his head held high, Ty crossed the stage and received his high school diploma.

As he flipped the tassel on his cap, the entire family jumped up, clapping and cheering, Autumn loudest of all. Next year, Ty would join her at community college—at least for one quarter—until she graduated with an associate degree in psychology.

Without homework, she hoped to have time to cook again. In the meantime, Mrs. Volkes, the new housekeeper, did a wonderful job.

"This is almost as cool as when you and Cody got married," Justin said.

"I'm really proud of Ty, but nothing will ever top our wedding."

Cody leaned down for a quick kiss. As always, Autumn went weak with love.

The boys rolled their eyes and broke into grins.

Autumn laughed. She had everything she'd always dreamed of—a husband who was the love of her life and four adoring sons.

The boys didn't know it yet, but six months from now, they'd become big brothers to Autumn and Cody's baby. Cody hoped for a girl, but Autumn didn't care, as long as the baby was healthy.

She'd paid back the merchants she owed, and Judge Niemeyer himself had offered to be a reference for her, if she needed one. He also gleefully reminded her that he was the one who'd steered her to the ranch in the first place.

Life was sweet.

* * * * *

REQUEST YOUR FREE BOOKS!
2 FREE NOVELS PLUS 2 FREE GIFTS!

HARLEQUIN

American ★ Romance

LOVE, HOME & HAPPINESS

YES! Please send me 2 FREE Harlequin® American Romance® novels and my 2 FREE gifts (gifts are worth about $10). After receiving them, if I don't wish to receive any more books, I can return the shipping statement marked "cancel." If I don't cancel, I will receive 4 brand-new novels every month and be billed just $4.49 per book in the U.S. or $5.24 per book in Canada. That's a savings of at least 14% off the cover price! It's quite a bargain! Shipping and handling is just 50¢ per book in the U.S. and 75¢ per book in Canada.* I understand that accepting the 2 free books and gifts places me under no obligation to buy anything. I can always return a shipment and cancel at any time. Even if I never buy another book, the two free books and gifts are mine to keep forever.

154/354 HDN FVPK

Name _____ (PLEASE PRINT) _____

Address _____ Apt. # _____

City _____ State/Prov. _____ Zip/Postal Code _____

Signature (if under 18, a parent or guardian must sign) _____

Mail to the **Harlequin® Reader Service:**
IN U.S.A.: P.O. Box 1867, Buffalo, NY 14240-1867
IN CANADA: P.O. Box 609, Fort Erie, Ontario L2A 5X3

Want to try two free books from another line?
Call 1-800-873-8635 or visit www.ReaderService.com.

* Terms and prices subject to change without notice. Prices do not include applicable taxes. Sales tax applicable in N.Y. Canadian residents will be charged applicable taxes. Offer not valid in Quebec. This offer is limited to one order per household. Not valid for current subscribers to Harlequin American Romance books. All orders subject to credit approval. Credit or debit balances in a customer's account(s) may be offset by any other outstanding balance owed by or to the customer. Please allow 4 to 6 weeks for delivery. Offer available while quantities last.

Your Privacy—The Harlequin® Reader Service is committed to protecting your privacy. Our Privacy Policy is available online at www.ReaderService.com or upon request from the Harlequin Reader Service.

We make a portion of our mailing list available to reputable third parties that offer products we believe may interest you. If you prefer that we not exchange your name with third parties, or if you wish to clarify or modify your communication preferences, please visit us at www.ReaderService.com/consumerschoice or write to us at Harlequin Reader Service Preference Service, P.O. Box 9062, Buffalo, NY 14269. Include your complete name and address.

HARI3

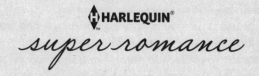

Wild for the Sheriff

by Kathleen O'Brien

On sale February 5

Dallas Garwood had always known that sooner or later he'd open a door, turn a corner or look up from his desk and see Rowena Wright standing there.

It wasn't logical. It was simply an unshakable certainty that she wasn't gone for good, that one day she would return.

Not to see him, of course. He didn't kid himself that their brief interlude had been important to her. But she'd be back for Bell River—the ranch that was part of her.

Still, he hadn't thought today would be the day he'd face her across the threshold of her former home.

Or that she would look so gaunt. Her beauty was still there, but buried beneath some kind of haggard exhaustion. Her wild green eyes were circled with shadows, and her white shirt and jeans hung on her.

Something twisted in his chest, stealing his words. He'd never expected to feel pity for Rowena Wright.

She still knew how to look sardonic. She took him in, and he saw himself as she did, from the white-lightning scar dividing his right eyebrow to the shiny gold star pinned at his breast.

Three-tenths of a second. That was all it took to make him feel boring and overdressed, as if his uniform were as much a costume as his son Alec's cowboy hat.

"*Sheriff* Dallas Garwood." The crooked smile on her red lips was cryptic. "I should have known. Truly, I should have known."

"I didn't realize you'd come home," he said, wishing he didn't sound so stiff.

"Come *back*," she corrected him. "After all these years, it might be a bit of a stretch to call Bell River *home*."

"I see." He didn't really, but so what? He'd been her lover once, but never her friend.

The funny thing was, right now he'd give almost anything to change that and resurrect that long-ago connection.

Will Dallas and Rowena reconnect? Or will she skip town again with everything left unsaid? Find out in *Wild for the Sheriff* by Kathleen O'Brien, available February 2013 from Harlequin® Superromance®.